# Julianna's Choice

The Stone Wolves
Book 1

Davina Guy

Publisher's Note:

This is a work of fiction. All names, characters, places, and events are the work of the author's imagination.

Any resemblance to real persons, places, or events is coincidental.

Solstice Publishing - www.solsticepublishing.com

# Julianna's Choice

## Davina Guy

For Terry. You've stuck with me through thick and thin, and although it took a few tries, I finally got it right with you.

# Chapter One

Thane Stone kissed his sleeping wife's forehead, gently pulled the hair away from her eyes, and tucked the blanket around her. He then tiptoed through the house, trying not to disturb her or his two daughters. The irresistible pull of the full moon snatched him from his slumbers, as it always did, but tonight he had work to do – wet work.

Sensing a change in the pack's mentality, he knew it was now or never. *Was Malcolm getting to them?* Rule through fear was Malcolm's motto and the weaker members soon fell in step with Malcolm's commands. As the Alpha-wolf, it was Malcolm's responsibility to keep the pack safe and to ensure they followed the "rules" – of which there were only three:

*1) Never kill a member of your own pack, or harm their family in any manner.*

*2) Never kill a human—unless the Wolfen court orders it.*

*3) Never allow a human to know what you are. (A human possessing this knowledge allowed the only exception to rule #2)*

Thane was a young man when Malcolm turned him and he quickly moved up the Wolfen ranks to become Malcolm's right-hand man. But as the years went by, the darkness in Malcolm grew into an insane lust for the kill. Malcolm no longer held to any of the old laws and traditions.

Thane began locking himself in during the change, wanting no part of the pack's bloody rampage. But Malcolm grew more and more bloodthirsty, until one night, he led the pack on a hunt. They massacred four campers and two children on Ice Mountain. They ripped the limbs from their bodies and feasted on their flesh, even sucking the marrow from their bones for dessert.

Thane had enough—he had to stop him. He tried to sway the pack against their leader, against murder, but Malcolm found out. On the weekend before the full moon, when Thane was away, the pack broke the cardinal rule, and attacked Thane's wife.

That violation forced many disaffected Wolfen to break away from Malcolm. They began their own pack, devoted to the old ways, and to ending Malcolm's reign of terror. Thane was their Alpha.

Tonight Thane hoped to end it once and for all. His spies uncovered the enemies' plot to attack a troop of camping scouts near the river. Thane's pack would gather at Devil's Knuckles, then converge on Malcolm's forces in the hollow below-- before they could pounce on the unsuspecting innocents.

Thane stepped through the door to his daughters' bedroom and smiled at their peaceful sleeping faces. His eyes watered at the thought of not seeing them again, but his young protégé promised to watch over and protect them if anything happened to him. That's the best he could do for his family. If he was to maintain his own humanity, Malcolm had to be stopped.

He reached into his pocket and withdrew two turquoise pendants. He placed one on each of his daughter's nightstands, then moved quickly, but silently, from the cabin toward his rendezvous.

# Chapter Two

"Damn girl, pick up the stupid phone already! Or turn down the volume – I'm tired of hearing it ring."

Julianna rubbed the sleep out of her eyes, and glanced at the alarm clock by her bed. *God, I'm so tired*! A full day of exams with only a twenty minute nap to recover wasn't cutting it.

She pulled herself across her bed and picked up her phone. *Lorelei.* She considered fabricating an excuse, any excuse to steal the reward of a few hours of sleep, but with the next ring, she sighed and answered the phone.

"Hey Lor, what's up? Is everything okay?"

"I guess it's nothing a full frontal lobotomy wouldn't fix."

"Oh come on. It can't be that bad… let me guess, Mom again?"

"Well, yeah, Mom. Who else? She's batty, Jules, battier than normal I mean. I'm at my wit's end. She waits for me to fall asleep, and goes sneaking out to the woods like before, doing her magical incantations or some shit, I don't know."

"Is she taking care of you? You know, during your moon cycle."

"Taking care of me? Hmm… yeah, if you consider keeping me locked up down there for two days as taking care of me! Then when she does come down to the basement, it's like she doesn't even remember I'm there. She made me miss my Senior Prom, Jules!"

"All right, I'm coming home. It's good timing with spring break, and I just finished my exams. I miss you anyway, and you don't need to be alone and having to deal with all that. I'll leave in the morning and should be there by mid-afternoon."

"No, you don't have to do that. I was hoping maybe you could just talk to her? She might listen to you, and I don't want to get her upset."

"Seriously, Lorelei? You know the two of us mix like oil and water. I'll be there. See you in the afternoon." Julianna hung up before her sister could argue further, and then dialed the gym. Frank Matheson, the owner, was a good guy to work for. He wasn't happy to hear she'd miss leading her classes, but Frank seemed to understand at least. Like everyone else, he had enough family issues of his own.

Julianna slipped into yoga pants and a halter and faced her kickboxing bag. She threw a round kick followed by an uppercut and a long series of jabs. Xena, her Yorkie, whined from the bed as Julianna completed her routine.

"It's okay, Xena, I'm not mad at you, baby." Julianna scratched her behind the ears. She pulled on her slippers and went out to the kitchen to tell her roommate Amy of her plans. Amy was at the sink, elbow-deep in pots and pans.

*Oh boy, I'm going to be a guinea pig for another bout of experimental recipes.* Cooking and new food fads were Amy's antidotes for depression.

"You need to get dressed, Julianna. I'd kill for that beautiful copper skin of yours and all, but you don't have to flaunt it, princess." Amy flipped her perfect blonde curls out of her eyes.

"This will work for around the apartment, I think."

"At least put on some decent clothes before everyone gets here."

"What? Who?"

"Come on, Julianna. Did you forget the guys are coming over tonight? And you tease me about being a dumb blonde."

"Crap, I did forget, but I'm going to have to be a party pooper. Sorry, but something has come up, kind of a family emergency, and I need to drive home tomorrow. I'll hang out for a bit, but I really have to turn in early tonight."

Amy scrunched her lips together and rolled her eyes toward the ceiling.

*Great, Amy's pissed, but tough, it can't be helped.* The mental release of a party might be exactly what she needed, but all she really felt up to right now was sleep, and she dreaded what faced her at the end of her journey tomorrow.

Julianna took a quick shower, dressed, and spent some time on her research paper before the doorbell rang.

Jen and Deborah arrived together, early of course, and Amy put them to work arranging the appetizers. Everyone looked up when Amy's treasured cuckoo clock began announcing the hour from the living room. Julianna knew they were all thinking the same thing.

"Where do you suppose they are?" Jen asked. "I swear, if John and Katie are late, the world will literally end!" In mid-cuckoo, a knock sounded on the door. Deborah cackled in delight when the newly "coupled" couple walked into the kitchen.

"We know you guys too well," Deborah said, still giggling.

"Well, I'd hope so. We've only been best friends since freshman year." Katie gave each of her friends a hug. "At least we aren't all finishing each other's sentences like you and Jen do."

Amy laughed. "Yeah, I think I need some new friends. It's a rare weekend when we aren't all hanging out together at some point. But speaking of which, I invited two new guys I met on campus over tonight. I think you'll like them."

"Fresh meat?" Katie winked at Julianna, who shot a look in Amy's direction (what Amy called her evil eye: one eyebrow hooded, and the other raised), but Amy responded with her sweet, innocent little girl smile, complete with matching dimples. *Two guys. Wonderful. That means one for Amy, and another one that she intends to fix me up with.*

Amy responded to the knock at the door and returned with a blond-haired man attached to her arm. She introduced him as Shane. He was tall, six foot or so, with a tight, well-built body, obvious even under his sports jacket. Julianna assumed he worked out, and wondered why she had never seen him at her gym before. He looked good, even if he was overdressed for a college party. A freshly pressed shirt and tie completed his dressed-to-impress ensemble. He smelled of money.

*Hell, I bet he even irons his socks. No, his maid probably does that.* She stared at his earring, a gold crescent moon, an odd decoration for a man's ear, but then, she didn't like earrings on men, or on women much either for that matter. Maybe that was the one thing she was old-fashioned about. Julianna preferred the strong, silent, rustic type, a real Marlboro man, but who knew? A different kind of man might change her luck.

As Shane got acquainted with the six friends, Julianna's gaze swept over him from his head to his brightly polished shoes, and unconsciously paused here and there. It was a shame she had to bail on the party tonight; it might have been fun. It had been so long since she'd had a break from her hectic life. She shook her head. *No, not tonight.* Julianna consoled herself with knowing how nice it would be to be home, at least to see her sister, and Lorelei needed her.

Julianna answered another knock on the door, and a sweet candy-like scent teased her nose. She did a double take when Chase Graves, one of her classmates in a few courses, strode in.

He was blessed with emerald green eyes, dark wavy hair, and chiseled good looks. No doubt young women were swooning over him before he even sprouted whiskers, although it was difficult to picture him without his well-groomed handlebar moustache. Chase wore his usual – tight-fitting jeans and a plaid flannel shirt that couldn't hide his trim and muscular body. He made casual look so hot, so male. In short, he was definitely her type, at least as far as appearances went.

Chase reached out and wrapped his arms around her in an awkward hug.

"It's good to see you again, Julianna."

Her mind drifted back to the classes they attended together, and the several coffee dates they went on soon after. They started out as fast friends. Then over dinner one night, he started acting possessive, relationship possessive. In all honesty, Julianna didn't trust her own feelings around him, even after their short acquaintance. She had even fantasized that someday, if the family curse was broken, she could really get used to having him in her life. He seemed to know every button to push on her heart – and body. For that very reason, she no longer let herself be alone around him. Sex had been off the table. Her body warmed at the sight of him, but she pushed the thought away. She couldn't allow herself that, not with the secrets in her family closet.

"I only want us to be friends," she'd told him after a weekend of soul searching.

"Very good friends, I hope. What about friends with benefits?" He flashed a white-toothed smile.

"I don't believe that's even possible. Friendships like that either become much more, or end altogether. I don't want either one."

"Then we are at an impasse, because I want, no, I need, more." His green eyes locked with hers before he'd walked away.

Julianna saw him everywhere around campus after that, always with a woman or two. She ignored him, and the more she did, the more effort he expended in the pursuit, the more he flaunted his female "friends" whenever she was near. Was he ever interested in her as a person? Were they ever really friends, or did he just play it up as a ploy to get in her pants? She did the math and it added up. He had played her. He wanted another notch on his belt, and the harder a woman was to get, the bigger the challenge, and that realization hurt. If he'd just been honest with her, she might have considered being one of those notches!

Amy greeted her latest guest and introduced him to everyone.

"We've met before," Chase said, looking at Shane.

Julianna noted the hostility passing between the two men. "So you guys know each other?"

"Yeah, we go way back." Chase's nostrils flared.

*God, men and their childish machismo,* she thought.

Xena strolled into the room, headed to her corner bed until she heard Chase's voice. She ran toward him, jumped up on the couch, and propelled herself into Chase's arms.

"Hey Xena, there's a good girl," he cooed in her ear.

Amy pulled Julianna to the side. "Okay, so I spotted you and Chase together in the library, and…"

"We weren't together, he just sat there. I didn't invite him."

"Well, I could see the way he looked at you from clear across the room, but I knew you weren't exactly interested anymore. I'd love to hear that story sometime. Anyway, after I finished checking out my books, I walked over to your table, but you were gone, so I asked him over tonight. He's so damn hot, but is it all right with you? I mean… well, you aren't into him, right? He's fair game? If he and I were to …"

"He's all yours, Amy. Rock his world, girlfriend!" Amy was right about one thing though, Julianna thought. Chase was hot enough to make a woman sweat just being near him, and suddenly her old desires raced through her body, electric, tormenting her. She had almost forgotten how tantalizing he was. No! If and when she needed her itch scratched, Shane's chances for a no-strings horizontal thrash were more probable than Chase's. Shane might at least be honest and appreciative afterwards, but a night with Chase would be a seduction built on lies, cheap and tawdry, and just another check mark in his little black book.

Amy gave Julianna a hug and a quick peck on the cheek. "Thanks, Jules. Shane's a good catch, too. I know he's a little stiff at first, but I heard his dad's filthy rich, and he only has the one brother." She winked at her, and Julianna rolled her eyes.

Julianna made nice, and enjoyed the conversation over light appetizers. She had a few drinks with her friends, both old and new. Chase flirted with all of the girls, even Jen and Deb. Either he hoped they were switch-hitters, Julianna thought, or else he lacked a lesbian notch on his belt, but she still felt his eyes following her whenever she moved.

Julianna thought of how people often grow into their names, but the name of the sluttiest girl she had ever met was named Chastity, and she knew a skinny, nerdy kid who went by Hunter…but Chase? His parents nailed it with his name.

Shane bantered with the other guests, but hung on Julianna's every word, making it clear she was the one he was interested in. When her glass ran low, he was quick to top it off. He was attentive and a perfect gentleman, perhaps too much so. She wondered how he would look in a flannel shirt and jeans – maybe even under her flannel sheets!

"Hello? Julianna?" Shane broke into her thoughts.

“I’m sorry, I was daydreaming.”

“Penny for your thoughts?”

“I’d have to give you change.” She laughed. “I’m sorry, what were you saying?”

“Your necklace, it’s beautiful. I love turquoise, always have.”

“It’s the goddess Diana, the huntress,” Amy interrupted. “It’s Julianna’s one concession to fashion. You will rarely see her without it.”

Shane looked up from the pendant to Julianna’s eyes. “A woman who looks like you needs very little in the way of ornamentation.”

She smiled. “Why, thank you, Shane. It was a gift from my father, who’s passed, and so it’s special to me. Besides, you know turquoise is the one essential adornment for all Native American women.” *This guy is quite the flirt.* At first glance, he seemed way too prissy for her taste, but there was another deeper element to the man, like when a book doesn’t match its cover. She felt a primal draw just as she felt when she was around Chase.

In a hurry to get to bed, or because the drinks helped her relax, Julianna sucked them down and felt lightheaded. She asked to be excused, gave the explanation of her family needing her at home, and said her good nights. She went to the kitchen for a glass of water, and Shane followed. He slipped up behind her and placed a hand on her shoulder. “Julianna?”

She turned to face him. “Yes?”

“I had a great time tonight, and I’d like to see you again soon. You said your family lives in Morton, and mine are in Ramsey. Do you think I could give you a call while you’re home? I’m going home over the break too, so maybe we could have dinner together? We are practically neighbors.”

“My father said all mountain folk are neighbors, and West Virginians especially so. Look, I’m sorry to cut it short too, Shane. I think I'd like it if you called. Just don't tell Amy. I'd never hear the end of it."

They exchanged phone numbers, and Shane gave her a hug. He bent over for a quick peck goodnight, and her arms circled his waist in return. As his lips touched hers, a quiver moved down her spine and settled at her core. She could feel the muscles of his chest pressing against her breasts through the thin cloth. Julianna was greedy for a human touch, preferably a human male's touch, and suddenly, this wasn't just a casual kiss between two new friends. She hugged him tighter and he lifted her to the counter. She felt Shane's hand slip under her blouse and stopped it before it could continue its advance. *Oh God, not this . . . not tonight.*

"No, Shane. Stop… I –"

"Oops, sorry, am I interrupting?" Chase asked from behind them.

"I assume that's a rhetorical question." Shane flashed his dark eyes at the other man. Chase glared back, did a slow about-face, and left. Shane turned back to Julianna, tried to step between her legs, and again snaked a hand beneath her blouse.

She grabbed it before it reached her breasts and brought her knees together. "Stop. I really like you Shane, but… stop. I'm not very used to alcohol, not to mention the fact that I just met you, or that all my friends are here. There's no way this is happening." She tugged on his arm, and he withdrew his hand. "I'm sorry. Good night." She hurried off to bed.

Sleep found Julianna, despite the flash heat Shane had stirred in her, and the incessant ramblings of her troubled mind. When she heard the creak of the door's hinges, and Shane stepped inside, she knew she was dreaming.

He pressed his muscular body against her from behind, spooning. One hand stroked its way over her back to cup a breast, then took a lazy tour of other parts of her body – kneading, and caressing. His fingernails trailed up and down the back of her thighs, and electric pulses coursed through her at each change of direction. She sighed.

His hand continued its journey along her body, always stopping just shy of more intimate places. *It's just a dream, Julianna. No harm done.*

She heard the rustle of his clothes, and his hands resumed their teasing caress. Her body trembled at his touch, a sweet agony.

He rolled her over so she lay flat, and his magic mouth followed the path of his hands. Warmth and tingling shocks flushed through her. She wanted him!

He kissed her belly button, then he moved up and kissed the nape of her neck, her lips, and nuzzled her ear.

Her eyes flew open, and she quickly surveyed her room. She felt like a child searching under the bed for monsters—but no one else was there.

It wasn't her imaginary passion that woke her, and no phones were ringing, but there were loud voices coming from the living room. When she heard a loud crash, Julianna grabbed her robe, and the baseball bat from the closet, before sneaking out of the room. Down the hall to the shared living room, she stared open-mouthed at the scene unfolding in front of her.

Shane got up from the floor rubbing his chin, and turned to face Chase. They looked like two battling bantam roosters with their shoulders squared off and chests puffed out. Fire burned in their eyes as each tried to stare down the other. *Oh God, this is just what I need, a drunken alpha male showdown.* Amy's treasured cuckoo clock lay smashed on the floor. She sat at the farthest point of the couch, eyes peeking through her hands, and mouth wide open. Their other friends were nowhere to be seen.

"Never fucked an Indian before..." Chase started, but shut up when Julianna entered the room.

Unbridled fire rose to her cheeks. He didn't want a notch on his belt for the number of women he'd screwed, but for the races he'd seduced. No wonder she was on his hit list. Native American women were rare enough on campus. What a sick shit! "What the hell is going on?" If you guys have a problem, take it outside. We don't need this crap in here. Are you okay, Amy?"

Amy nodded, and both men looked at her like children caught with their hands in the cookie jar.

"Sorry, Julianna, I –" Shane started.

She lifted her bat for emphasis, and she had no qualms about using it. Amy stirred from her trance, jumped up from the couch, and placed a hand on Julianna's bat.

"I'll take care of this, Jules. Go back to bed. I'll see you in the morning."

"I don't want to leave you alone with these assholes." Julianna glared at the two men.

"I'll take care of it. I know how to handle them. Go get some rest. You have a long day tomorrow."

Julianna retreated to her room, listened, and waited. At the sound of the apartment door closing, she lowered her guard and fell into a blissful sleep.

# Chapter Three

Julianna hit the snooze button three times before convincing herself to get up to face the day ahead. She knew things must be rough at home for Lorelei to call her for help.

She packed her bags as she considered the implications. Her mother casting her Wiccan spells again was not a good sign. It took too much out of her, mentally and physically. Helena's last attempt to cure Lorelei resulted in a suicide attempt, and landed her in the psyche ward for two weeks.

As she pulled her shower curtain open, she remembered she was out of shampoo and crept into Amy's bathroom to borrow hers. There was no indication of the evening's drama written on Amy's face. She snored away with the latest pop tunes playing on her radio.

*I have to tape her sleeping one of these days*, Julianna thought with a smile. The guttural pig grunts and bird chirps would be an instant hit on social media!

Between the music and snoring, Julianna didn't hear the shower running until she pulled open the bathroom door – at the exact moment when Shane stepped from behind the shower curtain.

"Shane!"

"Julianna!" He snatched at a towel to cover himself. "This isn't what it looks like!"

"I'll bet!

"No, Julianna, wait a minute!"

"I don't care, Shane. Have a good time!" She slammed the bathroom door.

"What's going on? Are you okay, Jules?"

Julianna stalked back to her room, ignoring Amy's shouted semi-conscious questions, and threw on some comfortable traveling clothes. The shower would just have to wait until she arrived home. She closed the snaps on her luggage, and it dawned on her that she was pissed for no good reason. Shane owed her nothing. She barely knew him, and dreams didn't count! But still, Amy was her friend, and Shane was set up to be her hook-up…

Amy sat waiting for her on the couch. "We have to talk," she said, stiff-lipped.

"You can have him too, Amy. Shane and Chase, they're both all yours."

"I can imagine what's churning through that pretty black-haired head of yours, princess, even though I'm pretty sure I don't want to know, but Shane slept on the sofa last night, not in my bed. He had too much to drink, and I made him stay – yes, despite what happened. Look, the sheets and blanket are still on the sofa. He asked if he could use the shower this morning. Notice I slept in my flannel jammies? Not seduction attire, wouldn't you agree?"

"Damn, Amy. I'm sorry." Julianna felt like a chastised child.

"You should be. I'm hurt that you thought I'd do that, especially after that foolishness between them last night, and what was said. You should have seen Shane just now, though. He scooted out of here like a scalded cat."

Julianna's face still burned, and she thought of Shane's face flushing in embarrassment, although when she peeked through her finger-covered eyes in the bathroom, he had nothing to be embarrassed about!

"Thanks. I'll make it up to him, I promise, but I'm late. I'll call you later."

"What? Make it up to him? Wait, Julianna. You don't need to… about last night …"

"Tell me when I call you. I have to go." She hustled from the apartment, not wanting to waste any more time thinking about Chase, or Shane either. It was tough enough the past few months keeping Chase's body out of her thoughts, whether awake or dreaming, but his comment last night cured her loins of any remnant of desire. Besides, she really was behind schedule.

The scenery along Interstate 68 never failed to give her pleasure. Even Xena seemed to be touched by it, as she stood on her hind legs gazing out of the passenger's side window.

Some people loved the mountains in early spring, when they could see the trees and wildflowers in bloom. Others crowded the back roads for a view of the changing leaves in fall. Julianna loved it in any season, but late spring to summer was her favorite time in the mountains. The hills and valleys were more private then, and it was also when the mountains came fully alive, swollen with verdant life. No matter how long she lived there, it always drew her in, and no matter where she settled, West Virginia would always be home.

Knowing Shane was a native Mountaineer made him all the more desirable, but the need to keep him, or any other man, at arm's length had not changed. How do you tell a prospective beau that your werewolf father was killed by his pack when he tried to stop them from taking human lives? Or that your witch mother was bitten in retribution? Surely they'd enjoy the part where your sister inherited the curse while still in your mother's womb. They'd love that, all the way to a padded cell at the looney bin! Maybe she could just say, "Oh, so you want to meet my family? Fine, but let me warn you, my mother's a witch, and my sister's a bitch."

After the two-hour drive, and numerous unanswered calls from Amy before the cellphone signal was lost, she turned onto the dirt road, and the cabin loomed straight ahead. She heard them as soon as she opened the car door.

"The moon is waxing, and almost full, Lorelei. You are susceptible now. The wolf's pull is getting stronger in you, and your teeth have already started growing this cycle!"

"You only want me locked up so you can go running through the woods casting your ridiculous spells! I love you, Mom, and I appreciate what you are trying to do for me, but your silly spells aren't helping me – in case you haven't noticed!"

"You only want to be free so you can find a dog boy to hump! You're like a bitch in heat now, Lorelei. You know that. You think I can't smell it on you? That's one benefit I got from the wolf's bite. What's worse is every wolf from here to Pocahontas County can smell you too."

"Oh my God, I will be so glad when Jules gets here."

Eavesdropping at the door, Julianna waited for her mother's response.

"*If* she comes, you mean? I don't know why you bothered your sister at college. She is no longer a part of this. She has a life of her own, and is free to do as she pleases. Maybe she'd still be family if she…"

The heat rose in Julianna's face, and she threw open the door. The other two women turned as she entered.

"Jules! I knew you'd come!" Lorelei leapt up and hugged her sister.

"If I what, Mom? If I'd not been safely tucked away in my bed when the wolves attacked you? Or if I'd been the one growing in your womb instead of Lorelei? Then we'd be a family? I'm so sorry I missed those golden opportunities for family bonding."

"If you didn't betray and abandon your family, Julianna. Watch your tongue, girl. This is my house!"

Julianna turned her back and stalked outside. She walked the trail that wandered through the woods behind the cabin until she heard Lorelei calling her name.

When Lorelei caught up with her, she thanked her for coming.

"C'mon, Sis. Don't let Mom ruin our time together. It's been too long since I've seen you."

They walked back to the cabin hand in hand, and prepared a quick dinner over which few words were spoken, just like in the old days. When they cleaned up the dishes, Helena threw a handful of unwashed utensils into the sink and faced her oldest daughter.

"Why are you even here, Julianna?"

"Lorelei is a young woman now, and she needs me. I don't want to see you drive her away with your overprotective, passive-aggressive bullshit. You can't keep her locked up forever, keeping her 'idle hands' busy with Cinderella work."

"I am at peace with my future. I know I'll die old and alone, and everyone will desert me. I've come to terms with that. But until then, I am the head of this family, and I know what Lorelei needs – the cure I'm seeking, and the basement room until I do."

Julianna shook her head. "I understand the need during the full moon, but she's fine until then. She can control it, and I'll keep her safe during the early transition times. I won't be distracted by having to cast any spells, and I don't need to call on any supernatural entities to do my bidding!" She glared at her mother.

"Do as you will, Julianna. You always have since you were fouling your britches." Helena threw her dish towel on the counter and left the cabin, slamming the door behind her.

"Well, that's the last we'll see of her tonight." Lorelei frowned and dried the last dish.

"Sorry, Sis. Come on, let's take a walk to the river." Julianna spotted the dog. "Xena, come."

Xena pranced ahead of them as they walked along the well-worn trail that led to the swimming hole the sisters swam in as children. Formed at a bend in the river, it ran tranquil and deep. A large flat-topped outcropping in the middle of the pool provided a spot to sunbathe or to just sit and enjoy the view.

"I need a swim," Lorelei said.

"That's a great idea, let's run back and get our suits."

"This isn't the big city, Jules." Lorelei laughed, and then yanked her T-shirt over her head, dropped her shorts and underwear, and dived in. Julianna couldn't help but notice her sister had grown into a woman since she'd been gone.

"Come on, Jules! Did you turn into a prude in your old age?" She splashed water in her sister's direction, and dived toward the rock bottom. Julianna stepped to the water's edge and looked to the left and right. They had skinny-dipped here as children, but they weren't children anymore.

Julianna paused as Lorelei's head bobbed to the surface. She felt self-conscious about her body – even around her sister – and what if someone saw them?

"Holy shit, do you think I want to see your tits?" Lorelei gave out a girlish giggle.

Julianna had forgotten werewolves could read minds, or at least see the images another person felt. The curse was stronger in her sister now. She'd have to guard her thoughts.

"What the hell!" Julianna slipped out of her clothes. She scanned the steep rock face across the river before jumping in and getting a sudden reminder of how cold the pool was. The frigid water sent shivers up her spine. Dipping her head underwater, she twisted and dived for the bottom. The swimming hole was ten feet deep during normal water levels, and clear as glass.

She swam in lazy circles. Once the shock of the cold water wore off, it felt so good. No pool in the city could match this! The exercise warmed her as she floated, carefree and alive.

"Glad to see you are still wearing your Diana pendant. It shows that some things haven't changed at least." Lorelei touched her own matching pendant and they climbed up on the "sunning" rock to dry off.

"Yes, it's the last thing Dad ever gave us."

"So, what are the boys like at college, Julianna?"

"Talk about changing the conversation." Julianna laughed. "I don't get to meet many, between my college courses and leading the classes at the gym. I usually just hang out with friends when I have any spare time."

"Come on, don't be so damn coy. You know Mom keeps me under lock and key, literally. I'm like some frickin' vestal virgin. Can't you share a risqué tale or two?"

Julianna hesitated and then took a deep breath. "There's a guy I'm sort of interested in. The best guys are either taken, or are intent on sowing all their wild oats before they leave college." She pictured Shane, naked in the shower, and Chase's face popped into her head uninvited and unwanted.

"Hmm, a pair of guys after you, huh?"

*Damn werewolf senses.* "No, one of them has some weird sex quest thing going, a mission to seduce every non-Caucasian woman. For his memoirs, maybe. I do think Shane is a good guy though, but nothing serious. That will never happen with this family." She forced a laugh.

"Is that why you don't want to be a part of this family? Why you haven't been home?"

"You know how Mom and I left it, but I will always be here for you, Lorelei. I promise. *You* are my family!"

Lorelei smiled before quickly glancing over her shoulder toward the rock face.

"What did you see?" Julianna asked, looking in the same direction. "An eagle?"

"No, but something…" Lorelei stood and brushed dark sand from her chest.

"God, you've grown up, Sis. Those things are pretty impressive."

"Well, I would hope I'd grow up some in the – what – two years you've been away? This isn't all me. They just get bigger when, well, you know…" She curled back her lips to form a clown-like smile, and her prominent canine fangs flashed. "That's when the guys really start clawing all over me."

"Most girls refer to other more mundane problems when they talk about their time of month." Julianna's eyes darkened. "But unwanted advances? I won't have that, Lor. Who's been pestering you?"

"Not entirely unwanted, just… I don't know… too intense I guess, but they all back down when I say so. I think they're a little scared of me, as well as turned on by my wolf."

"It's starting earlier, huh? The moon's pull on you?"

"Yeah, some I guess. Hey Jules, watch this." Lorelei smiled again, lifted her arms out to her sides, and rocked on the balls of her feet. Her breasts bounced as she slowly turned all the way around. She stopped and bowed toward the mountain. Her smile got larger.

"Lorelei, what the hell?"

Lorelei gestured toward the opposite side of the river. "See him?"

Julianna looked but saw nothing. Then the sun reflected off of glass. *Binoculars?* "Oh great, a peeper perv! Stop doing that, Lorelei! Let's get out of here."

They sprinted for the bank and their clothes. On the way home, they laughed like two young children, with Xena on their heels.

"I had no idea you were so brazen!" Julianna said and smiled as they reached the cabin.

"That felt good. During this phase of the moon, just smelling a boy's sweat gets me horny. Brushing up against one drives me batty. It felt so sweet to be the one doing the teasing for a change."

"Well, there's no way the pervert could climb down from that cliff to follow us, not in one piece anyway. No harm done, I guess."

"God, I missed you, Jules." She gave Julianna a hug.

# Chapter Four

The man placed the binoculars back in their case, stood up from his rocky perch, and brushed off the back of his pants. His clothes weren't intended for the rigors of the mountains, but Julianna was worth it. *What a hottie!* Breasts as firm as apples, with succulent plum-colored nipples. Best of all, she didn't even seem to know how attractive she was, or with what ease and innocence she fanned a man's desire.

*She knows exactly what she's doing,* his father's voice spoke in his head.

He leaned against an old oak tree, twisted by the wind and rocky soil. He allowed his mind a brief moment to replay the scene he'd just witnessed. Lorelei had filled out nicely since he'd been away at college, and that body was made for loving. But Lorelei was already theirs to claim by her birthright; it was just a matter of time and convenience.

It was Julianna who had drawn him back home again. The pack had chosen him to be her protector—to keep her safe until the time was ripe—until *she* was ripe. He pictured her skinny-dipping, her long sculpted legs tensed at the moment she dived in. Her black hair stirred by the breeze, and of course her upturned breasts, twin lasers zeroing in on him. He felt the surge of blood swelling him.

If things were different with their families, he might even consider having her around to play with for a while, or maybe not turn her at all. Wouldn't his family love that, and he grinned at the thought. He toyed with the idea of climbing down from his roost, catching the sisters, and taking them both in the woods by their cabin. Soon, he thought, soon!

He knew Julianna well, her likes and dislikes, even her taste in men, though it didn't seem she knew that herself. He'd followed her for a long time now. It wasn't the first time he'd seen her naked and vulnerable.

How much had she heard at the apartment that night? His wolf senses were on high alert, but somehow she'd snuck in on them. His nemesis would pay for that awkwardness, and for his lack of respect. He growled at the thought, at the promise of revenge.

But then a broad smirk turned his face into a sinister parody of joy. There was nothing in his oath to prevent him from having a little fun along the way.

# Chapter Five

The next morning, Julianna was up before their cocky rooster greeted the new dawn. She knocked on her mother's bedroom door, hoping to reconcile with her. No sense making the visit any more divisive than it needed to be, for Lorelei's sake if for no other reason. But her mother was either in too deep asleep, or she just wasn't interested in any conversation with her.

She found Lorelei sitting at the oak plank table in the kitchen, sipping from a mug.

"Mmm, this is some good coffee, Jules. Want some?"

"Oh, yes. Please."

"So what's your plan for the day?" Lorelei poured another cup of the hot black pick-me-up for her sister.

"I thought I'd drive to town and grab a few groceries. As it's been made quite clear that I'm not exactly an invited guest, I plan to pay my own way."

"Think I could hitch a ride? A change of scenery would be nice."

"I don't know, it depends … do you think you can go a whole day without flashing anyone?"

Lorelei laughed, coffee spewing from her lips.

"I promise." She grinned and held up one hand in a boy scout's pledge, but crossed fingers on the other hand.

Xena ran over to Julianna with her leash gripped in her teeth. "I'm sorry, Xena, but you can't go this time. Some people are funny about having dogs in their grocery stores and restaurants." Julianna patted her head.

Morton was only a fifteen-minute drive away, and the small town showed little sign of change since Julianna's last visit. *It probably hasn't changed much since our parents were children, other than some of the names on the mailboxes.*

Two teenage boys approached Lorelei the moment they entered the store.

"Hey Lorelei, how are you doing? We've missed you at school."

"Hey Bobby, hey Mike. Yeah, Mom's had me tied up." She winked and smiled at Julianna with only her lips, concealing her teeth.

"We were just going to grab a pizza next door at M&M's. Want to join us?" Mike asked.

She looked in her sister's direction. Julianna raised an eyebrow in question. Lorelei nodded her head.

"Go ahead, Sis. If you guys don't mind, I have some shopping to do. I'll catch up with you next door. But don't forget your promise, Sis!" Julianna winked, and Lorelei's cheeks blushed.

It was amazing how much stuff they stocked in the small Mom and Pop stores. Everything from fresh-cut steaks and vegetables to fishing worms, DVDs, and the West Virginia favorite, pepperoni rolls. Julianna gathered what she thought she might need, along with a freshly baked cherry pie, Lorelei's favorite dessert. She then made her way to the checkout counter to pay, and a vaguely familiar figure caught her eye outside. She hustled to the window and saw a man stepping up into a red truck. It was too late to get a good look before he drove away, but the man looked just like Chase. Why would he be here? He wouldn't, her eyes were playing tricks on her, and she wanted him whitewashed out of her brain.

Men were different creatures, she knew, but she didn't understand Chase at all. She heard his uninhibited laugh in her mind, and saw his slightly crooked smile. When he spoke her name, it sounded like a prayer, an inspired hymn.

She remembered his impassioned argument with one of their professors defending native rights. Chase's fervor and moral outrage over the forced native schools and the Trail of Tears. She thought the two of them would come to blows before the argument was done. How could such a man be a racist? Was it all part of his master plan of seduction?

She thought then of the day he dashed into traffic to save Xena when she slipped her leash. Chase ran as if his mother never told him to look both ways, and the screaming of brakes and the wailing of car horns scared her as much as it did Xena, but Chase was fearless. He snatched the puppy up virtually from under a truck's tires, never breaking stride, and then trotted back to place the pup in her arms. The dog licked his face as if it was a bowl of ice cream while angry drivers shouted ignored obscenities at him. How could he be such a caring man one minute and so cold-hearted the next? She suspected an Oscar for best actor was in his future, but she was done thinking about Chase Graves. *I'm really done this time!*

Julianna threw the groceries in the car and peeked in M&M's pizza shop. Mike stood behind Lorelei, massaging her shoulders. Bobby sat by her, rubbing her left hand while she tried to eat a slice of pizza with the other, and craning his neck for a better view of her cleavage. The pizza, untouched except for the piece in her sister's hand, grew cold on the table in front of them. Julianna didn't think anything or anyone could come between a young guy and his pizza. Lorelei mouthed the words "Thank God" when she spotted her sister.

"Hey, Sis, ready to go?" Julianna asked from just inside the door.

"She's still eating her pizza," Mike said. "Would you like to join us? We have plenty."

"No, I'm finished." Lorelei stood up from the table. "That was a big piece I had. Thanks for the pizza, guys. I'll see you in school." She rolled her eyes toward the ceiling so only Julianna could see, and hurried to the door. The boys' eyes didn't leave her as she walked toward Julianna at the door.

"Geez, those two really have the hots for you," Julianna said as they drove away.

"Not really. Last week, they flirted with me a little, but nothing like just now. My stupid curse works on them too. Guys get even hornier around me than I do around them during this phase of the moon." Her eyes watered, and she wiped it away.

"I'm sorry, Lor. It has to be hard. Is Mom really any closer to finding a cure?"

"The only cure is killing the one who bit her. You know that, but Mom just won't admit it to herself. She has this guilt thing going. She figures she managed to cure herself, but passed the curse on to me."

"Mom wrapped the wound with dogbane leaves, and drank a tincture of dogbane root and holy water filtered through charcoal after she was bitten. Amazing it didn't kill her, or you both, but she didn't know she was pregnant with you. Maybe a stronger potion would have worked, but I don't think her home remedy did anything at all, except give her the runs for a week. I think her placenta absorbed the cursed blood, and infected you." It felt odd to Julianna, defending her mother, but it felt right too. Lorelei's disease was what fueled their mother's insanity.

Julianna's phone rang before Lorelei replied. She frowned, thinking it was Amy calling again, but did a double take when she recognized the phone number Shane had given her.

"Hi, Shane, how goes it?" she asked, trying to conceal her mood.

"Look, I'm just so glad Amy explained the situation with the shower the other morning. I felt mortified. Hey, I was in your neighborhood earlier. I asked one of your neighbors where you lived, but nobody was home. I left you a 'welcome home, sorry about the misunderstanding' bottle of wine on your porch. I hope you don't mind."

"Mind? No, that was very sweet of you, but the misunderstanding was mine." She thought how lucky she was that her mother hadn't been home.

"I'll be down your way again this evening. Think we could go out for dinner or something?"

"Dinner? I don't think I can manage that tonight." She didn't want to leave Lorelei alone. Tomorrow night the moon would be full.

"Go, Jules! Go!" Lorelei whispered, waving her hands.

"Thanks for asking, and I promise to call if anything changes," she assured him.

"I hope you can work it out, Julianna. I'd really like to see you. Until then, goodbye."

Lorelei frowned at her when she hung up. "Now you're ticking me off, Julianna."

"I can't leave you alone tonight."

"Bullshit! I know why you act like little Miss Goody Two Shoes around me, all virginal and untouched. I know that act is for my benefit, but I have a grip on this thing. I'm eighteen now. I already feel like shit because it is my fault that you can't, or won't, have a real relationship. Go to dinner with that guy, please? Do it for me?"

"Next time, I promise."

"Right, during the new moon, no doubt. You don't trust me, and that's bad enough, but…" Lorelei started crying.

"Come on, Sis, it's okay."

"No, it's not. If you have to become someone else when you visit me, no wonder you never want to come home. Before long, we won't even be sisters anymore. I can't lose you, Jules!"

"That will never happen." Julianna pulled over to the shoulder of the road. "I mean it, kiddo, you're stuck with me." She held her little finger out for a pinky swear, and Lorelei grabbed it with her own.

They drove home after the tense moment passed, and hurried to get the groceries put away. On the kitchen table they found a hastily scribbled note from their mother: "Lorelei, I'm going to collect some herbs, and I have to look into something else, but I'll be home before dark. I'm so close to the cure I can taste it!"

"Guess I'll be reading bible passages and watching her dance around waving her incense burner again tonight. Maybe something different, like the time she slipped me a sleeping pill. I woke up tied to a tree in the woods, stark naked, while she tried to call demons to come rape me. She read somewhere that their seed would kill off the wolf poison."

"Oh my God, Lor…"

"Hey, it doesn't matter. Mom's a fruit cake, but she has no real powers, thank God! She'd never really hurt me, and she means well, even in her craziest moments. But now you have no excuse not to have dinner with your boyfriend."

"He's not –"

"Shut up and call him, or I swear I'll never call you for help again. Besides, if you stay, you and Mom will just fight anyway."

Julianna thought about it. On the one hand, she knew her sister was right. She also knew their mother would keep a stricter eye on Lorelei than she would, no worries there. On the other hand, Lorelei would have to put up with her gross, even if harmless, rituals. They'd survived many years of it together, and she wanted to avoid any conflict with her mother for now. That needed to wait until Lorelei graduated and moved in with her.

Julianna walked out to the porch, found the bottle of wine as Shane promised, and poured herself a glass. "Sweet," she said, and drank it down quickly, then noticed the note attached to the bottle: "Hope we can share this together soon. With affection, S."

"Sorry, Shane, too late." She poured herself another glass. Julianna relaxed, and recalled the dream of Shane's hands stroking her, his hard muscles pressed against her. She wondered if being near Lorelei was taking its toll on her libido too.

"Call him then," Lorelei said with a smile. "I'll lock myself in my room and won't let Mom in. I have the only key, and the doors are pretty stout. Trust me for a change, Julianna."

The combination of her raging hormones, the warmth of the wine, and her sister's logical pleas, especially her plea for trust, proved too much. She stepped out to the porch to call Shane. He sounded surprised to hear her voice, but happy to hear her plans had changed. They agreed to meet at a new place at the halfway point between their towns called Wolfe's Country Diner. *How appropriate.*

Julianna left earlier than needed, unsure exactly where the new restaurant was located, but she still arrived a few minutes late. She didn't see Shane in the parking lot, and none of the other vehicles were occupied. She stepped out and peered in the window of the diner, but didn't spot him. Not wanting to go in alone, she went back to her car and waited.

Fifteen minutes passed, and Julianna realized something had come up or more likely, she'd been stood up. It wouldn't be the first time. She started the car, but as she backed up, a sports car pulled in and blocked her exit. She blew her horn while looking back in her rearview mirror. Shane leapt out of the car and ran to her window.

"Fancy meeting you here, beautiful lady. I'm so sorry I'm late. Dad sent me on some errands that took longer than I expected."

"That's okay. Consider it a small part of my making up for that misunderstanding the other morning." She winked at him, and he laughed, then opened the car door for her.

# Chapter Six

The menu was more extensive than Julianna anticipated, but she ordered a light meal and a glass of wine. Shane did a great job of ensuring her glass was never empty. After a few glasses, she was glad she hadn't opted for a large dinner. She didn't follow the old-fashioned nonsense about a woman needing to pretend she didn't have an appetite, but she had a different kind of hunger tonight. She didn't enjoy romance as much on a full belly.

In the restaurant's light, Shane looked different somehow. A heavy growth of stubble adorned his face, but it was more than that. He looked more dangerous, and that made him even sexier.

"I was glad you called me back, Julianna. I was looking forward to another boring night at home with the old folks. God love 'em, but I can only play so many games of Scrabble." He looked down at the table and shook his head.

"Maybe we can make tonight a little more entertaining for you."

He jerked his head up, saw the smile. "Anything would be more interesting. What did you have in mind?"

"Don't get the wrong idea, Shane, but I would like to get to know you better, maybe make up for the misunderstanding the other morning."

"That works for me." Shane stopped picking at his food and took large bites, gave them a cursory chew or two, and swallowed.

She laughed. "Slow down, Shane, you'll choke yourself."

"I know, it's a bad habit of mine." He shrugged. "So how do you know Chase?"

*Great, Chase again.* "We had a few classes together and went out a few times."

"He's kind of a strange guy, don't you think?"

"He is, well he *was*, a friend. I wouldn't call him strange, any more than any other male creature I've met. Maybe more of a Romeo than most – he really likes the ladies – but that's about it." *What is wrong with me? Why am I defending him?*

"Really? I thought he was gay."

"No way! Women hang on his every word, and off of both of his shoulders too."

"Yeah, he was like that in high school, but I thought it was all an act. We weren't the best of friends then either. He's been a thorn in my side since I beat him out as quarterback in our senior year."

"So you knew Chase in high school."

"We're both from Ramsey. You didn't know that? But please, enough about Chase Graves. You'll make me jealous."

"You brought him up, Shane. Was he a racist bastard then?"

Shane's face blushed. "Huh? What do you mean? What did Amy tell you? I'm not too sure about her. She comes across as a bit of an instigator."

"Amy's left a few messages on my phone, but we haven't connected yet since I left. I've heard that kind of ignorance before. I just didn't expect it from Chase."

"I really don't know what to tell you. Like I said, we weren't exactly the best of friends."

"Okay, so let's talk about you, then. I didn't notice how white your smile was before. What do you use?"

He kept his lips together as he gave her a sheepish look. "I was hoping you wouldn't notice, but I'll come clean. I bought some whitening stuff to impress you tonight, and I fell asleep on our couch. This is pretty embarrassing."

She liked his honesty and gave him a sweet smile. "Don't be embarrassed. I'm flattered." She looked past him, trying to spot the sign for the rest room. A tall dark-haired man stood with his back to her as he paid his check at the cashier's counter. She caught a glimpse of a full mustache as he went through the door. Was it Chase, or whoever the guy was she saw earlier? She thought of the hillbilly jokes she hated. The ones about shallow gene pools, and everyone being related, but this guy had to be Chase's cousin at least. He even walked with Chase's slow, confident stride. She watched to see what vehicle he got into, but he walked out of her line of sight.

"Hello? Julianna, are you wandering off on me again?"

"Sorry, I thought I spotted someone I knew. I'm back, and all yours." And she meant it. She felt light-headed and uninhibited. The attractive man sitting across from her was causing a stirring in her nether regions. *The wine!*

Shane held up his finger as the server passed their table. "May I have the check, please?"

The tires on Shane's sports car squealed as he left the parking lot, and Julianna followed behind him in her car. She didn't want to leave the vehicle unattended, and she'd learned long ago not to leave her transportation – her exit strategy – in someone else's hands. Shane knew of a safe, secluded spot up on the mountain where they wouldn't be disturbed.

Julianna told herself it would be an opportunity to get to know him better, but her body told her something else. She thought she could trust him, but if not, the pepper spray in her purse wouldn't be far away.

Shane turned off the pavement, and his tires threw rocks catching traction on the dirt road before coming to a stop. He hurried from his car, opened Julianna's door, and led her, hand in hand, down a narrow, worn trail to a rocky overlook, high in the mountains.

"It's beautiful here, Shane," she said, after sitting on a blanket Shane had brought from the car.

"*You're* beautiful." Sitting down next to her, he stroked her hair, then leaned over and kissed her. His hand wandered over her shoulders, then he reached for the buttons of her blouse and plucked them open, one by one, kissing the flesh exposed as each was undone.

"No, Shane—slow down. We're just getting to know each other."

"I'm sorry, Julianna, I got carried away. Maybe we could just relax, have some wine, and talk?"

"Okay, but I need to go easy on the wine. I'm woozy from what I drank at dinner. I admit I'm a lightweight, but if I didn't know better, I'd think someone slipped me a mickey."

Shane laughed as he got up and walked back to his car to retrieve the wine and paper cups.

"This is the best vintage from my father's stock—homemade elderberry." He opened the wine and poured them both a Dixie-cup full.

Julianna stared up at the stars and sipped slowly from the cup.

"Look, Shane. There's Polaris, the North Star. It's the first star my father taught me."

"Where?"

"Do you see the Big Dipper there? Follow its top two stars across and down. See?" Julianna's finger directed his eyes to the points she described.

Shane leaned over to better locate the star, and wine sloshed from his cup onto Julianna's shirt.

Julianna stood too quickly and tripped, light-headed. Shane caught her, "I'm so sorry."

"Never mind, it's an old shirt anyway." She slipped it off of her shoulders and tossed it to the ground.

Shane held his hand over his eyes and laughed, peeking between his fingers.

Julianna tried not to join in. "Stop it, Shane. My modesty is perfectly well preserved, thank you very much. Bikinis provide less covering than this."

"You are so beautiful. A bikini or a ball gown, you'd do justice to anything—or nothing, I suspect."

"Easy, big boy, but thank you. You're not so bad yourself."

Shane held out his hand and helped her back down to the blanket. His lips found hers, and Julianna did not resist. Hungrily, they tasted each other.

"Ummm. That's nice," she purred, knowing how men liked sexy sounds coming from their women.

As Shane tried to entice her passion, Julianna's mind slipped away to another time and place. *Why does mom hate me so?* She remembered when she first left home, her mother slapping her and calling her a whore. Why did she…*not now Julianna!*

Shane brought her back to the present as his ardor increased. His kisses became too intense, too forceful. He pulled her tighter into his arms. His sharp nails dug into her back. *Geez, Shane, trim your damn claws.* His labored breath heated her neck. *Suck it up. It's not his fault you aren't into this.* Her thoughts slid to Chase and the last night at her apartment, and the discovery of the truth about someone she'd once considered a friend.

"Oh why, Chase?"

"Who?" Shane growled.

*Dear God, did I really say his name out loud?* "Shane, I'm so sorry. It's not what you think."

She felt him pulling away from her.

"Shane, I'm sorry. Really, I…"

He shook his head and frowned, his eyes as dark and dull as coal dust. He picked up her shirt and wiped the sweat from his brow, then threw it at her. He stood and walked to his car.

"Wait, Shane!"

"Call me when you get over that son of a bitch, or just don't call at all." He got in his car and sped away.

"Jerk!" she yelled as his taillights disappeared from view.

She tossed her soiled shirt over the cliff. It was her favorite blouse and would wash clean, but she didn't want it anymore. She didn't want to be reminded of this night every time she opened her closet door.

Julianna cursed, then gritted her teeth, puzzled over what had happened. Saying Chase's name was so stupid! How could she do that? She was only thinking of how Chase had hurt her. She wasn't imagining it was him she was with. But how would Shane know that? She knew she ruined the night for him, but he could have at least listened to her explanation!

For an hour she sat in the dark until her buzz faded, thinking of the events of the past few days.

A month was as long as she allowed any man in her life. No relationship would survive the knowledge of her family, or even inspire enough trust to share its secrets, but she had hurt Shane tonight. That she didn't like, even if he did overreact. She thought how she always seemed to have something to apologize to him for. Maybe he would give her a second chance.

Damn Chase Graves! She'd crossed him off of her friend list, but he still found a way to foul up her life. He was a bastard even when he wasn't trying to be. *Then why do you still think about him?*

She stopped the car on the cabin's gravel drive and sat there, trying to quell her anger at Shane, at Chase, and at herself. Men! She heard wolves in the distance as she snuck into the cabin in her bra and pants.

Sleep did not come easy. Tomorrow night, the moon would be full.

# Chapter Seven

Julianna slept longer than she intended, and a cup of coffee and a shower were her immediate priorities – in that order. Lorelei sat sipping from her own cup of caffeine in the kitchen, and smiled when her sister walked in. Julianna noticed Lorelai's canine teeth were much longer.

"Did you have a good time?" Lorelei asked.

Julianna playfully rubbed her sister's ear. It was fuzzier today, and looking closely she saw the barely perceptible pointed tip. "You look like an elf."

Lorelei slapped her hand away. "Yes, and my legs and pits are hairy, although I shaved them yesterday, and yes, even my butt cheeks are furry. Is the inspection over, or do you want to see my butt too?" She stood and hooked her thumbs in the waistband of her pajama bottoms, glaring at her sister.

"Wow, aren't we little Miss Sensitive today? Okay, I get it. Sit back down."

They sat without speaking for a few minutes, allowing their tempers to cool.

Lorelei broke the silence. "So, tell me all about your date last night. Shane, wasn't it?"

"Yeah, Shane, and not very good. I don't think I'll be seeing any more of him."

"Really? I could smell him on you when you crept past my door last night. The girls at school say even bad sex is better than no sex, and I know all about no sex. So…?"

"It's complicated, but I screwed it all up."

"What did you do? Giggle when you saw his teeny little wee-wee?"

Julianna couldn't help but laugh. Lorelei had a perverse way of cheering her up.

"No, Lorelei, and I hardly know him, so get a grip on your hormones and your overactive imagination. Actually, it was worse than that. Another guy's name popped out of my mouth when we were in the middle of making out. Well, he was the one putting the moves on me. I just couldn't get into it."

"Then what's the prob, Jules? Maybe you're just not into the dude."

"Yeah, maybe. That was bad enough, believe me, but it gets even worse. The guy's name I said is his sworn mortal enemy or some stupid macho guy foolishness. They've been rivals since high school."

"He'll get past it, he's a big boy. He is a big boy, right?" More giggles from the sexually repressed sister.

"That's not even a little bit funny." Julianna bit her lower lip.

"Why? Did you swear everlasting devotion to this Shane guy or something? So what if it's another guy who pulls your trigger? What's the big deal? You're a free woman."

"He doesn't pull my trigger and I don't want him, period. I don't even like him!"

"Umm, yeah, right. The lady doth protest too much, methinks."

"Very funny, Lorelei, I don't want to talk about this anymore." She rubbed her teeth over her lower lip as her face flushed, and her eyes watered.

"Hmm, little Miss Sensitive," Lorelei said.

Julianna sipped her coffee and stared out the window.

Lorelei put her hand over her sister's and rubbed her knuckles. "Guess who didn't come home last night?"

"Oh, no! Mom didn't come home? You were here all night alone? Were you all right?"

"I was great. I opened my bedroom window and humped every wolf boy in the tri-county area. I had no idea there were so many, they just kept coming and coming – no pun intended."

Julianna shook her head and clicked her tongue in disapproval. "You're a nut, sister of mine, but I'll bet you didn't mess up by calling out Rover's name when you were making out with Lassie!"

"Jules, Lassie was a girl, and I draw the line at she-wolves. Well, today I do, but maybe not tomorrow."

Julianna grinned and did an eye roll. "It will be so great when you graduate. I haven't laughed so much in a month of Sundays. I can't wait until you come back with me."

"I appreciate the offer, but I'm staying here after I graduate."

"What? Why? Is Mom pulling a guilt trip on you?"

"No, it has nothing to do with Mom. It's me. I can't keep on living like this, and I'm not going to ruin your life either."

"You wouldn't be – "

"I would, and I appreciate the fact that you would do that for me, but I'm done. I've had enough of living like this. I get the hots for a guy, and I don't know if it's a real attraction or the wolf in me. Lord knows I can't act on it, because once my cherry's gone, my monthly transition would be into a total Wolfen instead of just having extra furry girl parts, sharper teeth and pointy ears. If I left with you, or went anywhere else, they'd be there too, waiting for me. Plus, I'd never have a chance to get rid of this curse."

"What are you planning to do?"

"Let me show you."

Julianna followed her to her room. Lorelei stepped over to the closet and pulled aside some clothes to reveal another door. She slid it open.

"Mom didn't want me to take shop class, said it wasn't feminine, but I'm quite the carpenter now. Have a look."

She handed over a flashlight and Julianna peeked inside. A pegboard held three pistols, two shotguns, and a rifle. Boxes marked as ammunition with explosive warning labels were stacked knee-deep on the floor. A very shiny axe and two hunting knives completed the arsenal.

Julianna stood with her eyes wide, jaw agape. "What is this? And what did you do with my little sister? This is so not you!"

Lorelei laughed. "I bought the knives and the axe, but the rest were Dad's. I found his cache. But you're right, it's not me, it's you."

"Huh?"

"I asked myself what my big tough Amazon of a sister would do in the situation I'm in. I thought about it for weeks, and this is what I came up with. See, you did rub off on me some after all these years."

"What are you planning to do, play Rambo or something?"

"I'm going to kill the fucking wolf who bit Mom, and get free of this curse!"

"And if he gets you instead?"

"That's not going to happen, but if it does, I'd join the pack, and be a bitch-wolf once a month. Not my idea of a happily-ever-after ending, but I'm done straddling the fence and wishing for a real life, a normal life."

"Why wait until you graduate?"

"If I succeed, I'd have high school behind me, and I can start college. At least I'd have that. If I fail, it wouldn't matter, I guess."

"I don't see the difference."

"Look Jules, well…I'm scared to go it alone. I knew you'd come home when I graduate, but now you're already home, and spring classes are done you said and I hoped…"

"Don't the bullets need to be silver?" Julianna pointed to the ammo boxes.

"Reloaded with silver. It's amazing what you can get on the Internet nowadays."

"I need another cup of coffee." Julianna went back in the kitchen. She spotted Shane's bottle of wine, pulled the cork, and poured the rest down the drain. She didn't want anything that potent again for a long while, if ever.

The sisters enjoyed the rest of their day together, their conversations focused on simpler, safer things. They went for a walk along the river, ready to slip into the woods if they saw or heard anyone approaching. It was quiet in their corner of the world though, and no one got close enough to see the subtle changes in Lorelei.

"Are you ready?" Julianna asked just before dusk back at the cabin.

"Ready as I'll get."

They went down the stairs to the basement, to the room prepared for this night of every lunar cycle. The walls were made of solid four-inch blocks. The door consisted of oak studs bolted together, each of them two inches thick by six inches wide. The only source of light was a pair of tiny windows below the ceiling—fortified with inch thick steel bars. Even a fully changed dog-wolf, as their father was, could not escape the enclosure.

Lorelei sat on the "throne" as she called it. A throne built of solid concrete with chains embedded in it.

"Jules, would you stay with me? You'll have to hook me up if you do." She held up her arms as if in handcuffs.

"I thought it embarrassed you. That you liked to be alone when it happens."

"I do, but I'd like you to stay this time. I want you to see me. Maybe it will help you understand."

Julianna nodded, and locked Lorelei in by her wrists and ankles. She dropped into the recliner their Mom used when their father went wolfy. She felt uneasy, never having seen the change before. She had no idea what it would do to Lorelei. Was it dangerous?

"I promise I won't hurt you." Lorelei said.

# Chapter Eight

An hour passed with no changes in Lorelei, and little conversation between the sisters. What was to come weighed heavily on their minds. Julianna's eyes slid shut, and her head dropped down, then jerked up again, down, up, and down again. The dimness of the lighting, and the dead silence in the tomb-like room, lulled her to sleep.

Xena growled a warning, and Julianna's eyes shot open. Lorelei's nose had widened, darkened as if tanned, and her ears were elongated. The light hair above her lip had grown out.

"I'm sorry I fell asleep on you."

"Is okay," a deep guttural voice, not quite her sister's, said.

Lorelei's hands stiffened, seeming to lose their flexibility as her fingers became claws. She bit her lip, and a slow trickle of blood swelled and rolled down, dripping from her chin. A single tear slipped from her eye, and it too fell to her blouse. Xena growled, and then whimpered as she retreated to the farthest corner of the room.

There was no skeletal change in Lorelei like in the movies. Rather, her muscles convulsed and pulled her arms, legs, and back into what would be very uncomfortable or painful for a "normal" human being. Buttons popped on her blouse, and fabric ripped as muscles expanded. If this was the partial, virginal variant of the werewolf transformation, Julianna didn't want to see the full-blown effect, and she didn't want Lorelei to experience it either!

More blood seeped from her sister's mouth as her fangs grew to full length.

As quickly as it started, her face relaxed, the change complete. Julianna knew she was less hairy, less contorted than a full wolf. Only her fangs exhibited total transformation, and they were fearsome. She could still see her sister in the beast she'd become, but no one catching the smallest glimpse of this Lorelei would think her part of the normal, natural world.

"Jurr-els…" Her sister's beast eyes glistened with pools of moisture.

"I'm here, Lor."

"No pity, Jurrels," she growled.

"Pity you? I don't envy what you've been through, and I'd take the curse from you if I could." She leaned over the throne and kissed the top of her sister's head. "I'm taking the summer off, and we'll get the bastard who did this to you. I swear it!"

Lorelei's beast growled from deep in her chest. Her lips peeled back, exposing massive fangs.

"What? I thought you wanted me to stay and help." Xena began to bark.

Lorelei sniffed the air, then heaved her body upwards from the throne. With a violent motion, she swung her head to the side, and snarled. The top of the beast's head slammed into her sister's eyebrow, knocking her to the floor. The red of her own blood colored Julianna's vision.

"What the hell, Lor?" Then she heard the howls outside the cabin. The wolves from Berkshire County had arrived, acknowledging Lorelei's change. Tooth and claw bit and scratched at the doors in frustration, unable to meet their carnal needs, to make her one of their own.

Lorelei strained against her chains, thrashing and yanking at them in vain. Julianna noticed small cracks where the chains attached. The throne had proved itself over many years against her father's power, but were the cracks there before? Had the anchors weakened with time?

Her sister's violent rage increased in tempo with every whine or growl from the werewolves outside. Xena snarled at the ceiling, and bared her teeth as she again retreated to the corner.

Julianna heard breaking glass. Windows were the weak part of the cabin's defense. Heavy paws ran on the hardwood floor above her head, snorting in gusts of scent as they discovered the basement door. Their bodies hammered against it, and they growled in protest.

Lorelei gazed at the door of her prison, licked her swollen lips, and turned her yellow eyes on her sister. "Jurr-ells… Turn…loose!"

"No! I won't!"

Lorelei ground her loins against the stone of her seat. Writhing, growling, and humping the air. In her contorted form it might have been funny, a caricature, if it hadn't been so horrible, and if Lorelei wasn't the one trapped inside the beast.

"Peez, Jurr-ells!"

Julianna turned her head to hide her tears. Another body crashed into the basement door, and she heard the wood splintering.

*Boom! Boom!* Julianna jumped to her feet as a gun roared above. The snarling of the werewolves tortured her ears, and the walls shook from the clashing bodies slamming into them.

*Boom!* One of the creatures whined in pain. *Boom!* Another squealed. Then she heard a woman's scream. *Mom? What should I do?* She was unarmed, and she couldn't open the door of their cell. They'd get to Lorelei!

More screams, and another shot rang out. *Mom's alive!* But it was a male's voice that yelled at the wolves now. Padded paws ran through the house and then there was quiet.

Julianna sat in silence, except for the thudding in her chest, and pressed her finger to her lips for Lorelei to do the same. Did she understand? Who was in their house? Someone with the same agenda as theirs? Kill all the werewolves? If so, she couldn't let him see Lorelei as she now was. He'd kill her too… but their mother was up there!

She heard bodies being dragged across the hard floor. Then someone stepped toward the basement door. Julianna heard a male voice, and strained to hear the words.

"Helena…failed Thane," was all she understood, before hearing footsteps moving away from the door and fading away.

For hours, Julianna clutched the door of their cell, listening for any further conflict from the floor above them.

The faint light of pre-dawn made its way through the windows before Julianna felt safe enough to move. Lorelei, now changed back, slumped on the throne. Julianna released her chains and unlocked the door.

"I'm so thirsty, Jules."

Julianna poured a glass of water from the basement sink and cradled her sister in her arms, doing her best imitation of their mother's lullabies until she slept. Then she snuck out, ready to assess the damage of the night.

Climbing the basement stairs, Julianna stopped to listen, but heard nothing. It took all of her courage to unlock the door and turn the knob. She pushed on the door, but it only moved a few inches. She pushed harder, but whatever blocked her exit didn't budge.

"Let me help," Lorelei said from behind her. "Oh no, look!" She pointed at the pool of blood seeping under the door.

"Watch out!" She squeezed past Julianna and threw her weight against the stuck door. It creaked, bent out from the top, and with the next hit, broke free. Lorelei spilled forward and landed face first on her mother's bloodied remains. She screamed.

# Chapter Nine

They knelt beside their mom and brushed the hair away from her face. Blood dried in pools around her body from her many wounds. She had fought bravely, like a warrior, but the gash at her throat had finished her suffering.

"Who did this, Lor?"

"Huh?" Her eyebrows knitted together. "The wolves killed her, right?"

"Yeah, but who or what do you smell? There's wolf in you."

Lorelei stood up, looked again at their mother, and bit back a sob. She filled her nose with the air, and a puzzled frown took over her face.

"Well?"

"I don't know." Lorelei sniffed again. "It smells like wet dog of course, that's everywhere, but something else, from when we were kids.... I know, do you remember when Mom took us to the movies in town? She always bought us candy. It's like that."

"Licorice?"

Lorelei didn't answer, but reached down to open her mother's hand. Her fingers were closed over a long gold chain, and she gently pulled it free to reveal an old pocket watch. She opened it, and read aloud the inscription inside: "Thane, remember night falls quickly in the mountains. Our love, Mom and Dad."

"That's the gold watch our grandparents gave Dad," Julianna said. "He lost it a few years before he died. Where did that come from? Did Mom find it somewhere?"

"She never mentioned it to me if she did. But we have bigger problems than a watch mystery. What are we going to do? How do we explain this?"

"Calm down, there's nothing to explain. We didn't do anything wrong. Our mother was murdered, and I'm calling the cops. First we'll need to stack some storage boxes around the throne. They're sure to want to search the house."

"You're probably right, Jules. God, I'm glad you're here."

"At least there aren't any dead werewolves lying around." Her eyes got big and she rushed out of the house, returning a couple of minutes later. "None outside, either, thank God. If whoever was doing that shooting killed some, he must have dragged them out and hidden them in the woods."

"Why would he do that? Who is he?"

"I don't know, Lor, but we have to keep him out of it for now."

They practiced their story, and Julianna made the call. When the officers arrived, the questions began.

"Where were you when it all transpired?"

"In the basement hiding in our father's secure room. It's where he kept his valuables when he was alive."

"How did you know to go into hiding? Did you hear them coming?"

"Our mother told us to when the men started yelling and beating on the door."

"What did you hear after that?"

"Shooting, and screaming." Lorelei said. "Were there attack dogs?"

"We'll ask the questions, Miss. Why didn't your mother hide with you? Why did she stay upstairs and fight them?"

"We don't know." Lorelei started crying.

"And you, Miss, why did you say you were here?"

"Julianna is my name. I'm home on break from college."

"How many people do you think you heard?"

"Three? Maybe more."

"Was someone else shooting? Besides your mother?"

"We don't know, but it sounded like two different guns."

"Did your mother have any enemies?"

"Well, duh! Somebody killed her!"

The questions continued well into the afternoon before the coroner arrived and carted their mother away. When the last official vehicle pulled away from their yard, they finally relaxed.

The rest of the day was quiet for the sisters, a day to mourn in peace. They were talked out, with nothing left to say, and exhausted from the past twenty-four hours. They turned in early that night, knowing they were lucky to be alive, unlike their mother.

Julianna curled up in bed and thought of the many spats she'd had with her mother, the petty differences. Why mince words? They were knock-down, drag out fights, but she was still her mom. She died to protect them. Died still trying to cure Lorelei's curse. Now Lorelei's care and protection fell to her alone.

The morning came early, its arrival announced by the ringing of the phone. More questions from the police, with no answers. How could there be? What rational explanation could they find, or invent, to explain the manner of their mother's wounds, the wolf hair that forensics was sure to find, and the multiple shooters and shell casings on the floor?

Julianna desperately wanted revenge for her mother, freedom, and a normal life for her sister, but retribution wouldn't be dealt by the hands of the law. The killers' crimes wouldn't be weighed by the scales of justice, but at their own hands.

They drove to town to make the arrangements for Helena, and to find a final resting place where she could finally find peace from her demons, both real and imagined.

The sisters spent the next few days in a mental fog, going through their day on auto pilot. Speaking little, and trying to think even less. In their pain, they blamed themselves for every misstep in the mother-daughter relationship, but through it all they mourned her and their last connection with their youth.

The funeral was a small affair. Their mother didn't have many friends, preoccupied as she was with her family in her early life, and later, her mission to free Lorelei of the curse. Julianna noticed five or six kids in attendance who were Lorelei's age. Her own friends, Jen and Deborah, John and Katie, and Amy were also there. She had sent Amy a text to let her know what had happened, apologized for not having called her, and then ignored the phone again when Amy called to offer her condolences. She hadn't been up to facing that just yet.

She was surprised to see Shane, and even more so when he sidled up to stand behind her at the gravesite. She hesitated a moment, then offered him her hand. She noticed that he smiled as he looked past her to the fringes of the gathering. She followed his gaze and saw Chase standing there, returning Shane's stare. He dropped his eyes to the ground when they met Julianna's.

The preacher said nice things about their mom. Mrs. Helena Stone, the fine Christian wife and mother he called her, but Julianna doubted he'd ever met her.

Their friends formed a protective circle around the two sisters. Each of them waited patiently to express their sorrow, love, and willingness to help in any way.

"The family has requested that friends join them at the Morton Bar and Grill," the undertaker announced to the group of mourners.

Julianna walked toward the parking lot with her classmates before remembering her responsibility to the preacher. When she turned back to look for him, she saw Shane just a few feet away.

"You have no reason to want me there, but does the invitation extend to me as well? I'm so sorry, Julianna…about your mom and about the other night, I was a –"

"Not now, Shane, but I hope I'll see you at the restaurant." She gave him a quick hug, a friend's hug, and he jerked away, massaging his side.

"Sorry, I think I pulled a muscle or something."

"The preacher, I have to…"

"I'll see you in a bit then."

Julianna thanked the reverend and handed him an envelope with a contribution for his services.

She had managed to cope up until that point by telling herself, "You have to get through this, it's almost over," but now that she was alone, tears flowed, and a tortured sob escaped her throat. She scanned the parking lot through blurry eyes and spotted Lorelei chatting with two boys.

"You doing okay?" Chase's voice came from behind her.

She turned to see him kneeling over a grave with pulled weeds in his hand.

"As well as I can be."

Julianna started to ask a question, but then recognized the burial plot as her father's. Chase stood up, dropped the weeds, and brushed off his hands.

Julianna detected a strange scent, and she sniffed the air. She looked puzzled for a moment and then nodded slightly.

"I know what you mean. The air is especially fresh after the rain." Chase drew in a deep breath through his nose.

"It's not that, but… well, thank you for coming today."

"I wouldn't have missed it for anything." He shook his head. "I just meant I wanted to show my respect and support."

Julianna stared at the ground at his feet, not wanting to meet his eyes. She didn't need any extra stress today, not at her mother's funeral, but she had to know.

"Besides the fresh air, do you smell anything else, Chase? Kind of like licorice, maybe?"

"Oh yeah, probably. Good and Plentys." He laughed and pulled a box of the candy from his jacket pocket. "My weakness, remember? Well, one of them anyway. Want a handful?"

"No, thanks."

"I can't make it to the lunch. Shane and I …"

"That would be best, and thanks again for coming, Chase."

The sisters drove the half mile to the restaurant in silence, or if anything was said, it fell on Julianna's deaf ears. Other thoughts distracted her.

She'd not eaten at the small restaurant since she left for college, but not much had changed there either. From the homemade pies displayed under glass on the counter to the red gingham tablecloths, it was the image that popped in her mind whenever she thought of a country diner. Their friends were already there waiting for them, likely providing as many customers as the small place had seen in a week.

Everyone felt the need to hug them both again before they all sat to place their orders.

"Where's Amy?" Julianna asked Jen, sitting to her right, and noticed Shane was also absent.

Jen leaned over to whisper, "Potty."

A minute later, Shane and Amy entered the dining room together, red-faced and frowning. Two seats to Julianna's left were the only vacant chairs. Shane sat beside her, and Amy made a show of dragging the chair next to him to the far end of the table. She caught Julianna's eye, and nodded towards Shane with her eyebrows arched. She shook her head in disapproval. Julianna decided she'd have to give Amy a call for a private girl chat soon.

They caught up with each other's lives while they ate. Distracted, Julianna knew she wasn't the best hostess or conversationalist, but also knew they would forgive her under the circumstances. They chatted a bit more after their meals were finished, and then John stood.

"Julianna, Lorelei, again I'm so sorry for your loss. It's a terrible thing that's happened, and I will pray every night for your family's peace, and justice for your mom."

Murmurs of agreement came from the other guests and Katie said, "We should be heading back, John."

"Call if there's anything we can do," John said and escorted Katie to the door.

The rest of the mourners soon followed their lead, but Shane and Amy remained. Both acted as if they were waiting for something or an opportunity to be alone with her. Julianna hadn't attended any funerals since her father died. Did she miss some important step of social etiquette?

Lorelei joined them after the last of her friends left. Shane and Amy spoke to Julianna and to Lorelei, but seemed to be ignoring each other. What's going on with those two? Julianna wondered as she paid the check and returned to their table.

"I hate to cut this short, and we thank you so much for coming to be with us, but Lorelei and I still have some things to take care of."

"We certainly understand, Julianna." Shane bent down and kissed her.

Amy glared at him, fire shooting out of her baby blues. She grabbed a pen from her purse and scribbled on her napkin.

Shane fell in step behind Julianna, and touched her arm as she reached for her car door.

"When you're ready, and if you want to, I'd love to see you again," he said, his puppy dog eyes pleading.

Amy's approach interrupted Julianna's answer.

"Goodbye for now then," Shane said and walked away.

"I love you, Julianna." Amy kissed her cheek. "Lorelei, take good care of your sister. She's a princess, you know."

"Thank you, my Queen." Julianna smiled and climbed into the car.

Amy poked her hand through the open window. "When you have time." She gave Julianna a folded paper napkin and walked away to her car.

Julianna tossed the napkin onto the dashboard as Lorelei got in the passenger seat. She started the car and drove out of the parking lot.

"Was Shane that tall hunky guy?" Lorelei asked.

"Yes." "

"He didn't seem at all put out with you. Maybe because he thinks you'll put out for him."

"Wipe the smirk off your face."

"Yes, your most Royal Highness. There must be a good story there with those names."

Julianna shook her head. "That princess thing started during our first year, when we lived in the dorm. Amy, as you might have noticed, is rather well-endowed. She was in her leather phase then, and didn't take anything off of anybody. And still doesn't for that matter, but with that and the blonde hair, the girls nicknamed her the Viking Queen. She said with my figure and our heritage, of course, that I looked like an Indian princess. She watched too many Pocahontas movies, I guess. Luckily, neither of the nicknames stuck."

"Oh, I don't know, it may stick now, Princess!"

Julianna remembered the napkin. She pulled it open and read, “Texts aren’t going through, so call me when you have bars!! It’s important!!!”

Important to Amy? That could be anything from a new dress she bought to a new guy she’d met, and Julianna filed it away for future reference. More important to her was what she’d smelled in the graveyard. The same candy smell from her apartment the night of the party. The same smell lingering around her mother’s murder scene. Licorice! Was Chase at their house on the night her mother was killed? Did he murder her? Was he one of the werewolves she swore to kill?

# Chapter Ten

"Damn, Jules, let's do something, even if it's wrong!"

"There's not much we can do until the next full moon. Where would we start?"

"I'm just tired of sitting and waiting. It's been weeks now. I'm going stir-crazy. Cabin fever."

"The guns are clean. The belts we made will hold enough ammo to lay siege to a castle. We have our leather jackets to help protect us from being bitten. I think we're ready."

"What about that old book I found with Mom's stuff? Did you read that part where it tells you how to spot a werewolf in their human form?"

"I don't think I trust it. Is the lore real or is it fantasy? Besides, we can't hunt someone down because they have an aversion to being in the water. You, for example, are half wolf, and you're practically a fish! Or because they are quick-tempered just before the full moon cycle? Okay, I'll give you that one, but enjoying lots of meat and always thirsty, the length of their fingers and fingernails, unibrows, strange sleep habits? Who do you want to kill based on that?"

"What am I going to do?" Lorelei slapped her hands down on the table and buried her face on them.

"Huh? When?"

"Think about it! If the only time we can kill them is when the moon is full, when my blood is high, I'll be so horny I'll be more inclined to mate with them than shoot them. You know that."

Julianna had seen her sister's condition during the full moon and knew she couldn't be trusted then – even to help herself. Hunting the Wolfen on her own was her only recourse. "We'll think of something."

"We need to work out a plan soon. The full moon will start affecting me tomorrow. It has some already, and it's getting stronger, lasting longer." She shook her head as if to clear her thoughts. "I just need to get out of here for a while." She left the kitchen and returned moments later carrying a small bag. "I'm taking a walk down to the river. Maybe take a swim. See you later."

"Keep your tits covered up!" Julianna yelled, and the screen door slammed shut.

She retrieved one of her mother's old photo albums and curled up on the threadbare couch to reminisce. She smiled as the relaxing memories of happier times made her drowsy, and sleep took her.

She jerked awake as beams of sunlight hit her eyes. As the sun fell behind the trees, the light hit the window in a perfect slant to her resting spot. She wondered how long she'd slept. It seemed like minutes, but the anniversary clock on the mantle over the fireplace told her hours had passed.

"Lorelei? Are you back?" No answer.

"Lorelei?" No response. She figured her sister was swimming—hopefully, not without a suit again – and had lost track of time. *Kid sisters, you've got to love 'em.*

Julianna grabbed her walking staff and rushed outside to follow the trail through the woods. She didn't yell for her sister, confident she'd find her at the swimming hole, but as she approached the water, she heard voices.

"Mmm, you are beautiful," a man said.

"You're not too shabby yourself. Oh yeah, kiss me there. Ahh."

Was that Lorelei? Damn! Julianna listened, but she couldn't be sure. The couple said nothing else, only passionate moans and grunts escaped from behind the sunning rock. *Here goes nothing.* She tiptoed around the boulder to confront the lovers.

Chase! His shirt was off and he was curled up beside her bikini-clad sister, arms wrapped around her as his hand made lazy circles on her tiny bikini bottom, her hips wiggling in response.

"That feels good!" Lorelei squeezed his butt with both hands.

Julianna jumped out from behind the boulder. "What the hell are you doing?"

"Jules? What…"

Chase jumped up and turned to face her. Julianna swung her walking stick and caught him behind his left ear. He staggered back.

"Jules, stop it!" Lorelei shouted.

"What the hell is your problem, lady?" Chase held his ear as blood trickled down his cheek.

"My problem? You bastard!"

"Easy now," he said, as Julianna lifted her walking stick for round two. He held up his hand, palm out, and then looked back at Lorelei. "You said you were eighteen. You are, right?"

She nodded, and he shrugged his shoulders, as if to say the problem was solved.

"You're a dog! You couldn't get with one Native American woman, so you go after her baby sister? You really are a perverted piece of crap."

"What the hell are you talking about?" He took a step towards her.

She swung the walking stick again, but he jumped back and blocked its impact with his forearm. *What a shame.* She was going for a home run this time.

"Love the new moustache dye, Chase. You get so vain you couldn't bear that little bit of grey? Figure that will help you get with some young girl?"

"Chase? I'm not Chase, I'm…wait… Julianna?"

Julianna drew back her walking stick for another swing.

"Wait, Julianna. I didn't know she was Lorelei. She's really grown up." He backed away from her. When he was out of range of the stick, he turned, picked up his shirt, and trotted quickly away through the woods – down-river in the opposite direction of their cabin.

"What did you think you were doing, Lorelei?" Julianna thumped her walking stick on the ground for emphasis.

"Me? What were *you* doing? You could have killed him!"

"I'm protecting you, that's what. What were you thinking? You know what will happen!"

"Look, I didn't know you knew the guy, but screw you, Jules! You don't understand anything." Lorelei grabbed her clothes and stomped her way back up the trail toward home. Julianna let her anger cool for a few minutes before following.

At the cabin, she poured a glass of wine, needing the liquid courage for the confrontation with her sister. The bottom of the wine glass signaled the end of her procrastination. She walked toward Lorelei's room, only to hear the same sounds as she'd heard at the river. Did Chase have the nerve to invade their home after what had just happened? She hurried to the porch to retrieve the walking stick, then went back to Lorelei's room.

"Oh… ahhhh…"

She tried to turn the doorknob, but it was locked.

Julianna spotted a wide gap at the bottom of the door, and dropped down to peer through it. By laying on her belly with her head turned to the side, she was able to see the full length of her sister's bed. Lorelei was alone. One hand was rubbing a nipple through her top, and the other hand . . .

*"There's nothing wrong with that. It's natural. There's no man with her,"* said her conscience, her good angel.

*You know who she's thinking about, and she wants him too,* said her little devil's voice.

*She does not. And I don't either! He destroyed our friendship.*

*He's hot, and there's nothing wrong with fantasizing.*

Julianna quickly moved to her own bedroom and climbed on the bed. She tried to shut her brain down, but visions of Shane crowded her mind.

She imagined him with her now, holding her, telling her everything would be all right. His hand gently pushing her hair away from her eyes. His tender caresses…

She closed her eyes to give in to the fantasy. But Shane's image slipped away, and Chase was now smiling down on her. The same smile he had when saving Xena. Oh, Chase!

Tears flowed down her face. She gasped as anguish racked her body, and bit into her shirt to muffle the sounds of her pain.

# Chapter Eleven

Julianna went to the kitchen, poured herself another glass of wine, and took to the living room to wait for Lorelei. She felt sick to her stomach. Why couldn't she erase the images of Chase from her mind? Fantasy or not, how could she think of him at all, especially that way, after all he'd done? But wasn't that the point of a fantasy, to imagine doing what you'd never do in real life? Maybe Chase was a safe fantasy because she knew she'd never be with him. Still, how could he do what he'd done? With her own sister no less? Even in the worst of times, she'd always considered him a friend. There was no honor in that man, no decency. Was anything beneath him?

At least she had Shane now. Well, sort of. Chase was the last man on earth she'd consider sharing her heart or her bed with! That knowledge, coupled with having used him as her fantasy piece of meat – as he'd wanted to use her – she found somehow reassuring. Her finger marked an imaginary "X" in the air.

"Fantasy sex with a redneck Caucasian bigoted pervert. Guess I can cross that one off of my bucket list. Screw you, Chase Graves!"

"Lorelei, are you okay?" she yelled. Surely she was done with her daydreaming by now.

Julianna heard movement in Lorelei's room, then her door opened, slammed shut, and footsteps ran toward the basement door.

"What the hell?" She went down the basement stairs and saw Lorelei sitting on the throne with the chains attached to her wrists.

"Why are you down here, Lor? The full moon isn't for two nights yet. Is it getting that bad? That strong already?"

"What do you care? I'm shackled one way or the other, it might as well be down here!"

"Look Lorelei, if this is about what happened at the river, I didn't want …"

"You didn't want what? Me to have any pleasure, any semblance of a normal life? You didn't want to trust me? So, you know that guy, maybe you just wanted him for yourself. Is that what it is? He didn't act like he even knew you!"

"He knows me all right," she said as her face flushed. "And this isn't about me. Hell no, I don't want him, but you can't have him either, Lorelei. You know what will happen, and I'm sorry, really I am. I can't even imagine how much all this must suck for you."

"Look, Sis, I have to stay a virgin, I know that. But I don't have to be a lily white one. I've let guys make out with me a couple of times before when life got too intense, and I return the favor too – without letting them do the dirty deed. He knew from the start that was off limits."

Julianna dropped her head and shook it from side to side. "Okay. I guess you're right, maybe I jumped the gun a bit. But just so you know, it's not a matter of trusting you. I do trust you, but when I saw you behind that rock after you said the pull of the moon was getting stronger, I guess I overreacted."

"Duh. Just a smidge ya think?"

Julianna handed her the key to the locks and touched her cheek.

"I'm sorry, Sis. Please come upstairs when you're ready. We have to plan for the full moon. I've got something to tell you."

She sat on the couch waiting, still nursing her second glass of wine, when Lorelei came into the living room and plopped down next to her.

"Before you get started, tell me about that guy. He said his name was Jase, by the way, not your Chase. But he said I'd grown up, so how does he know me? How do you know him, and what's the big secret?"

"I know him from school. We even went out together a couple of times, but it didn't work out."

"You mean you wouldn't let the relationship work out. My curse shouldn't be the end of your life too, Jules. You're being stupid. Just remember not to bring them home during the full moon."

"That has nothing to do with it this time, but I remembered something at the funeral. Chase loves licorice, and he has a special craving for Good and Plenty. That remind you of anything?"

"You think he was here that night? I didn't smell any licorice on him today, and my sense of smell is pretty acute right now."

"Maybe he took a shower and brushed his teeth before he tried to hump my baby sister."

"Okay, so Chase is off limits for now and for me period. I didn't know about your history, even though I suspect, despite your denials, that you aren't finished with him yet. My God, Jules, he is so hot! Have you seen his pecs? Of course you have, but…" Julianna's brow knitted together, and Lorelei stopped short. "Okay, I'll stop, but by the way, quit the baby sister bullshit. It's getting old."

*I am done with him.*

"Sure Sis, if you say so. Anyway, what did you want to tell me?"

Julianna felt her shoulders brace as she prepared to tell her. "I can't take a chance on you hunting with me. You won't be in any condition for it, I know that now, and you must too if you're honest with yourself."

"No, Jules! I have to…you have to…"

"Lorelei, I can't."

"You can. I was looking through Mom's old books yesterday, and an old yellowed piece of paper fell out. A recipe."

"What kind of recipe? Mom's special meatloaf?"

"Nothing like that. There's herbs and dogbane root in it. A note in Mom's handwriting indicated it diminishes the effect of the transformation. I figure if it will help curtail a full wolf's change, it might really help me."

"Mom probably tried it out on you already. She was constantly pouring elixirs down your throat. What else you got?"

"I don't think she did, Jules. She wrote 'Last Resort/One Time Use Only' across the top of the recipe. There's death cap mushroom in it, like the ones under our hemlock tree. There was also a warning that it can only be administered while in the initial throes of the change."

"So you want me to give you a glass of poison, one too potent for Mom to even consider, just as your body is convulsing from the change?"

"No, well yes. But I know something that Mom didn't eighteen years ago. Silymarin."

"Silly what?"

"Silymarin. It's in milk thistle, and so far, studies show it works as an antidote to the mushroom's poison."

"So far, the studies show." Julianna paused for effect. "Really? I've never even heard of it, Lorelei."

"Do you think because you're in college, you're the only one in the family who can read? I think it's safe enough."

"No, it's too risky.

"If you don't help me, Jules, I'll figure out a way to do it without you, even if it's before my change. I swear I will."

“What does ‘one use only’ mean? That it can accumulate in the body, or that your body builds a resistance to it?”

“I don’t know. I do know this full moon is my only chance. Besides, what do I have to lose?”

“How about your life?”

Lorelei shrugged her shoulders, and her eyes watered.

Julianna finally understood the full cost of her sister’s curse.

# Chapter Twelve

"Wake up, Sleeping Beauty!" Julianna knocked on her sister's door. "I figured it was time I made the morning coffee for a change."

"I'll be right there, Princess Pocahontas," Lorelei answered with a yawn.

Lorelei crept toward the table, rubbing her eyes, and took a tentative sip from her cup. "It's not as good as mine."

Julianna flipped her the finger. "Tough, but we need to get a move on if we're going to gather all the plants and mushrooms for Mom's concoction. How much preparation is involved in that recipe of yours?"

Lorelei jumped up from the table and ran around to her sister, slamming her hip on the table's edge. "Ouch!" She threw her arms around her.

"Thank you, thank you, and thank you! I love you, Jules!"

"I'm not happy about it, but I understand, Sis, I really do."

"The recipe isn't hard, and I saw a patch of dogbane down by the river yesterday."

"I imagine you were playing botanist before you were, ahem, distracted by other pursuits?"

"Maybe." Lorelei gave her a wry smile.

"After our coffee, I need to pick up a few things in town. Do you think you can find everything on the list before I get back?"

"I've got it covered. You're not just making an excuse so you can go see Shane, are you?"

Julianna opened her mouth to make a smart comment, but stopped when she saw the worried look on her sister's face.

"No, I'll be quick, there and back."

"Thanks Jules. I really don't want to be alone for long."

In truth, calling Shane had crossed Julianna's mind. It might be her last chance to be with a man, or her last chance to do anything for a while, if not forever.

As Julianna drove to town, she considered their plans for the following night. Two young women against the werewolf horde? How many were there? Their numbers were thinned out some during the cabin attack, but how many were left? Would they come again? Assuming the recipe worked, would they still be drawn to Lorelei, or would they pursue easier targets? But the most important question: could Julianna count on her sister during the full moon?

The diner in town had Wi-Fi available, so she pulled in and ordered a coffee. Her tablet confirmed all Lorelei said about silymarin's use in treating mushroom poisoning, even though its use was not yet approved.

She walked across the street to the hardware store and consulted her shopping list: two machetes, duct tape, another hunting knife, rope, and dog pepper spray. A skinny, pimply young guy in a red smock helped her to find everything, although with each thing she asked for, he lifted his eyebrows a bit higher.

"Ma'am, are you all right?"

"I'm fine, despite the fact that you just called me ma'am. This probably looks strange though, huh? There's a stray dog in our neighborhood, and some of our shrubs are getting out of control."

He seemed satisfied, or perhaps relieved, at her explanation. Hopefully, he wouldn't be questioned by the sheriff if they were arrested for their upcoming full moon activities!

Julianna paid for her purchases and was accosted by the local Girl Scout troop as she left. She bought two boxes of the little mint cookies. They were Lorelei's favorite kind, and she hoped they would give her sister's spirits a boost.

Sliding the cookie boxes in the bag with her other items caused the bag to split, and its contents fell to the concrete sidewalk with a metallic clang. When Julianna knelt down to retrieve them, an extra pair of hands appeared.

"Quite an odd selection of purchases," Chase said. "Are you preparing for battle or something?"

"I just may be, and if so, you may be my first victim." Her eyes bore holes through him.

"Jesus, Julianna! What did I do now?"

"You have to ask me that? Just get the hell away from me, Chase." She stalked toward her car. He caught up with her as she struggled to tote her purchases without ripping the bag any further.

"Hey, wait up. Look, I took the summer semester off, and…"

"I knew that when I saw you yesterday."

"Yesterday? I must have missed you. But look, I don't know what's going on with you, Julianna. I don't know why you went so cold on me when we were going out, but now it's gotten to a whole new level. I know you're with Shane now, and I'm okay with that – maybe. I know I said I couldn't be just friends with you, but I'm willing to try."

"I'm just so happy you're fine with my seeing Shane. I can rest easy now. As for friendship, huh, little late for that, don't you think?"

"No, no I don't," he said as she tossed her bags in her trunk. She turned, and Chase had corralled her against the car. She pushed him away.

"Look, stud. I said all I wanted to say to you yesterday, but in case you weren't listening, I'm just not interested. I wasn't before, and I'm damn sure not since you tried to fuck my baby sister! Oh, and I'm glad to see you washed the silly dye off of your upper lip. It looked like a seventies porn star and as fake as shoe polish."

Julianna got in the car and slammed the door shut. Her window was open, and Chase continued talking.

"Lorelei? What the hell are you talking about?"

He sounded sincere. Did she give him a concussion? *Good!*

Chase pulled his father's silver compass out of his pocket, and started flipping it open and closed. Julianna knew it was a habit Chase had when uncomfortable. He leaned against the car's roof, and when she turned again to face him, she noticed his belt. There was a row of little cutout notches in the leather along the front edge, and one of them was fresh. She thought men only counted home runs, not just trips to first base. Oh yeah, he remembered yesterday all right!

"I really need to talk to you, Julianna. You might be in danger."

"Stay the hell away from me and my sister, or the only one in danger will be you. You have no idea the harm you could have done, you stupid shit!"

She backed up with Chase still trying to hold onto the top of the car. She put the car in drive, and then heard him say, "Jase!"

She didn't understand what was going on with Chase, but she wasn't afraid of him. Did he really think she'd have anything to do with him? Friendship even? After the events of the past month? Who knew what he'd do next and then conveniently forget all about it? How special was that?

Werewolves were enough to deal with. She didn't need Chase's insane antics on top of that. Unless… maybe it was the same problem. She wondered what the Viking Queen would do and pulled over to the narrow shoulder of the road. Amy was a bad-ass when it came to relationships, whether with males or females. She had a lot of experience and maybe she'd have some ideas about dealing with wolves too. Amy answered the phone on the second ring.

"Good God, finally! I didn't think you'd ever call me, Julianna. The least you could do is answer the damn phone once in a while when your best friend calls you."

"I'm sorry. You know cellphone reception is terrible in the mountains. Look, I have a problem …"

"Yes, I bet you do, and I also bet it's man-related."

"Well, yeah, kinda. Man, dog – guess it's all the same."

"Wow, that bad? What's going on?"

"It's Chase."

"Chase? Come on, Julianna, he's the least of your worries. He's your biggest fan. Now Shane…"

"No, you don't understand. Ever since my last night in the apartment, he's acted weird. I heard what the pervert said about me, and I guess he knows I know, but he even tried to seduce my little sister! Maybe he's pissed off because I heard him, and it's some weird reverse revenge. I don't know, but he's pissed me off."

"Damn, slow down and catch your breath, girlfriend. First of all, I don't know what you think you heard at the apartment, but –"

"You don't have to protect my feelings, Amy. I told you, I heard him. How he'd never 'done it with an Indian.' I guess I ruined his plans to make me his first conquest."

"God, you're a dumb ass! Shane is the one who said that, just before Chase knocked him down for it. Shane was so stupid and arrogant, he asked Chase why he hit him, and that's when Chase repeated what Shane said, just as you walked in."

"What?"

"Well, at least that explains why you were seeing Shane. I thought you'd lost your mind."

"So Chase wasn't the one who –"

"Look, Princess, that guy only has eyes for you, as they say. As far as seducing your sister, I find it hard to believe. I mean I saw her, and damn right, Lorelei is a gorgeous young woman and all, I'll definitely give her that, but I failed to get in Chase's pants, and I'm not without some seductive charms of my own. I damn near stripped on the couch for him. Hell, I would have if Shane wasn't there, but I couldn't drag Chase to my bed. It was all too humiliating."

"I saw him and Lor with my own eyes, Amy."

"Well, if you saw it, you saw it. Maybe baby sister is a better seductress than I am. Maybe I need to ask her to give me some pointers."

Julianna laughed. "Yeah, you really need pointers on that, all right. Think you could do me a favor though?"

"If I can. Name it."

"I don't have Internet at the cabin. Can you see what you can pull up on both of those guys, Shane and Chase? Something is weird with them, and anything might help."

"Oh yeah, I'd love to find out all their dirty little secrets. When I was little, I always wanted to be another Nancy Drew."

Julianna thought of nothing but their conversation for the rest of the drive home. Shane wasn't the one she needed to apologize to; Chase was, or he would have been if not for what he tried to do with Lorelei. He didn't owe her his faithfulness, though, and Lorelei wasn't resisting. *But he acted like he didn't even know me at the river at first, and his pretense of confusion just now in the parking lot? Would his lies never end?*

Chase was an oversexed pervert, and she'd made it clear to him they had no future together. Maybe his libido was out of control, and he was an odd sort of friend, but at least not an enemy. He defended her against Shane's racist comment, after all, or defended her race at least.

Amy, bless her heart, had exaggerated his level of affection for her. But still, maybe he wasn't just trying to score another notch in his belt. *So what do those belt notches mean?*

No matter if he didn't remember what he'd done with Lorelei, or if he did know and didn't care, something didn't add up. A startling thought that had lightly brushed the fringes of her mind came through dead center: Could it be that the moon's pull affected him too – because he was one of them?

If that were the case, it wouldn't matter if he were friend or foe. To save Lorelei, she'd have to spill his blood.

# Chapter Thirteen

As Julianna got out of the car back at the cabin, Lorelei walked into the open area of the woods that served as their yard. She had a bucket in each hand.

"I have enough goodies to make two recipes, in case we screw it up."

"Good job, Sis. Let me show you what I've bought." She popped open the trunk.

"They look nice and sharp." Lorelei tested each blade's edge. "But what good are they? Don't they have to be silver?"

"That's another job for you, along with Mom's potion. Remember the silver plating kit Mom ordered when she wanted to impress the neighbors? Hopefully it's still good, but it will have to do."

Lorelei laughed when Julianna pulled out the dog spray.

"This should come in handy. What's the rope for?"

"Snares. You were only ten when dad was killed. I doubt you'd remember, but he used to booby trap the woods around the cabin. The pit trap was my favorite, and might still be there, but I'll need to make new snares and deadfalls. They won't know what hit 'em when they come calling."

"*If* they come calling."

"You know they'll be here, and we'll be ready to greet them."

The pit trap was caved in with leaves and broken branches, but exactly where Julianna remembered it being. She scraped out all of the debris and inserted new sharpened stakes in the bottom, then used saplings and leaves to conceal the hole.

She was chopping down a pine tree for the deadfalls when Lorelei joined her, and she welcomed the help. It was hard, sweaty work. By nightfall, half of their traps were set, and they gratefully retreated to the cabin for showers.

The machetes and knives gleamed in the kitchen light. Four repurposed peanut jars stood on the counter filled with gooey fluid.

"Two tonics and two antidotes, just in case," Lorelei replied to Julianna's unspoken question.

"Having second thoughts? I wouldn't blame you if you were."

"No, I need to do this. It's my fight."

"It's our fight. You're all the family I have, baby sister. Oops, sorry about that."

"I'll forgive you – this time." She smiled, and her fangs glistened.

The day's labor had taken its toll on the women, who had no trouble falling asleep that evening.

Julianna felt as if she'd just closed her eyes for the night when their mouthy rooster sounded off.

"I should have bought gloves yesterday," she told herself, inspecting the blisters on her hands.

The morning coffee ritual was abbreviated. They wanted to finish up with their remaining chores as soon as possible. Julianna began with the axe, made a few swings, and then winced when a blood blister popped open on her palm.

"My turn." Lorelei took the axe from her.

By the time they were finished, they were both dragging butt, and they knew the night ahead would take all the strength they could muster.

"It's almost time," Lorelei said, and Julianna nodded.

They cleaned themselves up and took the potions to the basement. Julianna locked Lorelei in and waited. The change came on her much faster this time. She heaved on her chains as Julianna tried to pour the fluid down her gaping toothsome mouth.

Lorelei's beast snapped at her hand, and Julianna backed away.

"Saw-ree, Jurr-ells." Her head flew backwards, and she snapped at the ceiling.

"Now. Do now," she growled.

Julianna stepped forward again, mindful of her sister's teeth and managed to get the fluid into her mouth. Lorelei gagged, but swallowed. Nothing happened for a moment before she swung her head from side to side in agony and screamed in her monster's voice.

"Lorelei!" Julianna reached behind her for the antidote. Her sister's body shook and Julianna straddled her, uncaring about her jaws, as she struggled to force the saving liquid into her. Lorelei's head swung violently.

"No!" Lorelei snarled. Foam dripped from the corner of her mouth, and her eyes rolled to the back of her head.

"Lorelei, please!"

The convulsions slowed, and her features softened. Her muscles slowly relaxed. It was working!

Howls sounded in the distance. Xena scratched at the thick wooden door and added her own voice to the night. The pack was coming.

"I'm going to trust you now, Lorelei." Julianna released her chains. As the pack's howls moved closer, a wail ripped through the night, followed by yelps of apparent pain. *The traps are working!*

Werewolves now clawed at the walls of their cabin, just like before, but the bars they added to the windows, and the reinforced doors, held them at bay.

Lorelei showed no sign of life, and Julianna shook her.

"Snap out of it, Lorelei. Can you hear me?"

Lorelei's chin still rested on her chest. Her breathing was labored, but steady. Julianna felt her pulse, and it was strong. Lorelei felt feverish, and Julianna wet a cloth and wiped the sweat from her forehead. Lorelei reacted to the cold cloth by jerking her head up.

"Jules, I'm still alive. See, I told you it would work." She stood up, trembling but smiling.

"Easy, we'll go out when you're ready. Listen. The wolves are gone." Julianna wondered if the wolves were frustrated by their home's defenses, or if they were off in search of easier prey, but she knew they needed to get after them, and soon.

Lorelei began doing jumping jacks, demonstrating her readiness. They changed into their leather, strapped on their weapons, and stood at the front door.

Julianna thought about Chase then, the old Chase she remembered from when they first met—kind, gentle and supportive Chase, and felt no shame. She wished she could hold him, the way he was before she found out the truth about him. Before she knew he only wanted her as another feather in his cap and everything went wrong. His firm strong body, his strength fueling hers… but she'd casually tossed his friendship away when he got too close. What she wouldn't give to touch her lips to his! Did those same lips now conceal fangs? She turned to Lorelei.

"Ready?"

"Yup, now it's our turn." Lorelei reached for the doorknob.

# Chapter Fourteen

The women moved silently through the woods, guided by Lorelei's heightened sense of smell. The wolf pack moved along a deer trail toward a creek that fed the river. They weren't running, but they were werewolves, and even though the sisters were in good shape, they had to race to gain ground. They had more to spur them forward than just their next meal.

Lorelei stopped and held her finger to her lips. Julianna stepped toward her, testing the ground before she committed her weight. She didn't want the snapping sound of a breaking twig to give away their position. She leaned forward to place her ear close to her sister's mouth.

"They're just ahead of us."

"How close?"

"Maybe thirty yards. I don't hear any movement."

"Ambush?"

Lorelei nodded her head, and they pulled the pistols from their belts, one in each hand. Lorelei inclined her head and stepped forward. Julianna followed.

"Too quiet."

Julianna knew exactly what she meant. No owls hooted, no raccoons scurried through the leaves. Boulders framed both sides of the deer path ahead of them. *That's where they'll be waiting.*

Lorelei made a sweeping gesture to indicate she wanted them to split up, leave the trail, and work around the boulders.

"No," Julianna whispered. "We need to stay together."

Lorelei frowned, jerked her head in the direction she wanted her sister to go, then moved to the right. *Her senses are better than mine*, Julianna thought, and stepped off the trail to the left.

They moved slowly, one step at a time, guns at the ready, trying to pick up any sound. The night remained still as they made it halfway around the boulders, as quiet as a graveyard. Then Julianna heard it. A commotion on the other side of the trail. Then a growl. Lorelei!

She cut through the woods toward the guttural sounds of the wolves. She reached the largest boulder, and leaned against its rough face. She could hear them sucking the air through their enlarged nostrils – a wet slurping sound, as they tested the air for any scent.

Sliding her feet along the edge of the rock, Julianna leaned around the boulder and peered into the moonlit clearing amid the rocks. Five wolves were grouped in a circle with her sister at its center, and they were closing in. One had bloody matted hair on its side.

Lorelei's pistol roared once, then again. A beast fell heavily to the ground as the others pounced. Julianna jumped from behind her hiding place, but they were all around Lorelei. If she shot she might hit her sister!

The Alpha wolf, grizzled and larger than the others, held Lorelei pinned with one paw. With the other, he ripped aside her leather jacket as if it were paper.

Julianna had her gun sights trained on a spot centered between his shoulder blades. *Breathe in, then halfway out, and squeeze the trigger. Just like Dad taught me.* A mistake in aim could miss him completely. The bullet might pass through and hit Lorelei. Then the wolves would kill them both. The howling started all around them beyond the small natural arena. It started out soft, but gained in volume until it filled the night. *The woods were full of them!*

The bloodied younger wolf leaned in under the older wolf's back legs. Was he biting Lorelei? No, she made no sound beyond a whimper. He started backing away, pulling at something. The waistband of Lorelei's pants were in his teeth. They were trying to mate with her, and turn her into one of their own!

Julianna squeezed the trigger, and the big Alpha wolf fell beside Lorelei. The younger wolf grabbed onto her shredded jacket with his teeth and started dragging her toward the brush. Lorelei broke free and crawled away. Another wolf tried to climb on top of her.

Again Julianna pulled the trigger and the wolf fell. Over and over she shot at targets as more howling pierced her ears. They were everywhere! Wolf blood flew until she pulled the trigger on an empty chamber, and a sharp pain struck the back of her head. Her vision blurred, and the stars wavered in the night sky.

*Boom! Pop! Pop! Boom! Pop!* Lights flashed all around her.

*Did Lorelei get to her pistol?* Then the world spun and went black.

# Chapter Fifteen

Julianna awoke with the sense of movement. She was lying on her back on something, being dragged. Had the werewolves captured her? Where was Lorelei? She tried to sit up, but her head swam with pain. She reached up and felt something warm and sticky. Blood.

"Are we here, or somewhere else?" She knew what she wanted to ask, but the words didn't come out right.

"You're safe now." A man's voice. He sounded familiar, but she couldn't think straight. She squinted, trying to see who it was in the dark. His head…something wasn't right about his head. Cobwebs filled her mind.

"Do I know you?"

There was silence for a moment, then, "It would appear not."

"Where is Lorelei?"

Silence.

They hit a bump, and her body twisted. The stars danced again. She closed her eyes but it didn't stop the merry-go-round in her head. She tried to concentrate, to stop the spinning, and opened her eyes again. Lorelei's bloodied face lay inches away from her own! Julianna screamed, and darkness fell again.

She woke in her bed with a splitting headache. She felt her head, and the sticky blood had been washed away. She didn't remember getting undressed or even how she got home! There was a guy…

"Lorelei!" She ran to her sister's room and threw open the door just as Lorelei slid her feet to the floor. She was also cleaned up and partially undressed. A bloody bandage began at her throat and ended below her left breast.

"Thank God you're all right! What the hell happened last night?"

"I was going to ask you. How did we get home?"

Julianna shook her head. "I don't know. What do you remember?"

"I remember you shooting the furry beast that was trying to hump me! Then the one that was dragging me, you hit that son of a bitch right in the balls. He was bleeding like a stuck pig, but he limped off. I didn't think you were ever going to shoot. What took you so long? That wolf almost made me his bitch!"

"I couldn't get off a clean shot. They were all around you, and I was afraid of hitting you, but when things got ugly, I had no choice. Do you know what happened after?"

"When the big horny one fell on top of me, I tried to crawl out from under him, but he was too heavy. The more I struggled, the weaker I got. I don't think I passed out or anything, but maybe the mushrooms got to me. Or it could be that my wolf blood was too thin. I don't know. All I know is some guy with a hoodie dragged me out from under the wolf, and I was so weak, I couldn't stand. He handed me his water bottle and said it would make me feel better. That's all I remember until I woke up nearly naked, bandaged and bathed with no idea who or how."

"Did you recognize the man?"

"No, he had the hood pulled low over his head, and he had a scarf tied around his face."

*That's why his head didn't look right.* "Is that all you remember?"

Lorelei looked at her. "I do remember having a dream, and you were screaming."

"I did scream when I woke up and saw you."

"Thanks a lot, Jules."

"No, you were all bloody, and I thought you were…"

"I know, just teasing, and I would be dead if you hadn't been there, but we're okay… somehow."

"Let's get dressed. We need to figure out where we're going from here."

After donning fresh clothes, they gravitated to their conference room – the kitchen table – and settled down for coffee.

"How's your neck and boob?" Julianna asked.

"I changed the bandage, and it looks clean, but you'll be pleased to know I won't be flashing anyone anytime soon. My head is pounding, and I think I'm going to puke my guts out. Other than that, I'm just peachy. It sure could be a lot worse!"

"The mushrooms are still in your system. I'll get the antidote."

"You didn't give it to me last night? There's an empty jar of it on my night stand."

Julianna shook her head at the latest mystery and handed her the second dose. "I have to reset the traps and make sure they didn't leave any of their dead behind. If so, we'll drag them over to the pit trap and fill it in. We can set another snare or two instead."

Lorelei chugged the liquid down, made a face, and took a gulp of hot coffee. She stared out the window at the mountains. A tear beaded up on her lower eyelid. "Do you think we got lucky last night and got the wolf that bit Mom?"

"I don't know, but I sure hope we did."

"And if we didn't?"

There were too many wolves in the pack. Their mother's magic concoction was good for only one use. There was no way of knowing how many they'd killed, assuming the wolves removed the bodies. They couldn't fight them all. Their father died trying, as did their mother in a different way.

"Let's see what we can find out today. Maybe we can find some evidence that will identify some of them. Maybe there's some wolf hair in the snares, or blood on the spikes in the pit. Give us an idea of how many we took out."

"That elixir was one use only, Jules."

"I know, and that one dose has you looking like death warmed over."

"So what happens on the next full moon?"

"We'll think of something before then." But Julianna knew she couldn't do it alone. She'd have to take Lorelei far away. Maybe where there were no werewolves? If there was such a place, that's where they'd go, and pray the pack didn't follow.

It was a warm late spring morning, and the only hint of clouds was the mist rising off the mountains. They both loved this time of year, and being outside improved their outlook on life. Lorelei searched the area around the cabin for clues, while her sister went to investigate the traps. She was barely out of sight of the cabin when Lorelei called her back.

"Look at what I found! I know how we got home."

Julianna trotted back through the trees and found her sister holding herself up against the side of the cabin.

"You okay?"

"Um, just a little dizzy. But look!" She pointed to their mother's raspberry bushes, now pushed flat by two long poles. They lifted them up and out, revealing a roughly fashioned travois, wide enough for two slim women.

"Hmm, well that explains how we got here, but it sure would be nice to know who pulled that thing." Before she returned to the traps, Julianna insisted Lorelei go inside to rest.

"I can still help," she said. "I'll just move a little slower."

"I can't do squat if I'm worried about you passing out. I don't have time for this shit!"

Julianna waited for the cabin door to shut behind her sister, then worked her way back to the traps. *Lorelei will probably come back outside as soon as my back is turned*, she thought, and smiled. She glanced back over her shoulder, tripped over a rock, and fell face first into the woods' dark soil. She sat up to pry the rock from the path.

Something shiny caught her eye in the poison ivy vines. She thought of the angry blistered rash she experienced as a child, and carefully flipped the metal object out with a stick, then bent over to examine it. A silver compass. Her eyes grew misty. *Chase!*

# Chapter Sixteen

Events were forcing his hand, and he would have to make a game-changing move soon. Last night did not go according to his plans, but nothing ever did when it came to Julianna. He wondered how much she remembered. Did she recall who pulled them to safety? He might improve his standing with her by claiming the deed as his own.

Julianna proved herself to be as worthy an adversary as did her father before her. Lorelei was no slouch either, but that was to be expected. A mere Initiate perhaps, but Wolfen blood coursed through her veins, and the blood spore of the predator would not be denied. He felt drawn to Lorelei as well. When she achieved full wolf status, the two of them would be the only natural-born Wolfen in the pack. They would become the Alpha male and female, but Julianna would still be his. Sisters need to share, after all. *Sisters. Sweet!*

He let his mind wander, and pictured the three of them in his bed, naked of course. It didn't require much imagination, given their penchant for putting their assets on display. Lorelei bent over, her elbows on the bed, as she screamed in pleasure (or pain, as if that mattered).

Julianna's hands and mouth were everywhere, squeezing him, exploring, but her part was secondary, as it should be for the pack's sex slave. She was too strong to be subservient, and would make his life hell if he allowed her to be his mate, the Alpha female. It was no worse than she deserved for the way she treated him, and the grief she now caused him with the pack. And what a perfect revenge on her old man, having both his precious daughters become Wolfen sluts!

He grinned in delightful anticipation before he remembered. No time for daydreaming now. He needed to focus on his plan, and control his wolf until it was needed.

The sisters would be good breeders. Strong, smart, and loyal, all fine traits for the mothers of the next generation of Wolfen. Over time, the pack would beat down their annoying independent streak. No doubt it was because of their Daddy issues, he thought, but maybe he could use that to his advantage. He could be one fatherly son of a bitch if that would win Julianna's trust.

No, he thought, not fatherly. He could use their fond reminisces of their father to capture their hearts. He had many recollections of Thane, and he could relate those memories in any manner he chose. He could turn himself into a hero in their minds.

His old enemy joining the fight complicated things. Ripping out that bastard's throat would bring almost as much joy as turning the two sisters, but all in good time, when the pack was gathered. Soon he would reach out to Julianna again. He'd learned many tricks over the years, and concealing the daytime effects of the change was very basic stuff – Wolfen 101.

# Chapter Seventeen

*Why would Chase's compass be here?* If he was the one who helped them last night, as she hoped, he'd have no reason to be so far from their house. Dragging two bodies behind him, he would take the most direct route. But the wolves? They were all over their property, and evidence of their identities is what she searched for.

"Please Chase, just when I thought you might be a friend, just when I need a friend…please don't turn into my enemy now," she thought out loud. The trees did not reply, and she continued searching the ground and resetting her traps.

Long strands of dark fur were embedded in the rope fibers on four of the snares, though no carcasses were found. *Yes! Four down!* Several of the pit trap spikes were painted with canine blood, but there was no way to tell how many were killed. Multiple spears might have impaled the same wolf.

Back at the cabin, she discovered Lorelei sleeping on the couch, so she grabbed a book and her cellphone and took them to the front porch— the only spot with cell reception. She curled up in one of the Adirondack chairs with Xena in her lap, and dialed Amy's number. After four rings, the answering machine kicked on, then the beep.

"Amy, give me a call when you get this. I'm sitting on the porch with my head twisted to the north, and one leg in the air. I can get two bars that way. Call me!"

She opened her romance novel, turned to her bookmark, and the phone rang. Amy!

"Hey! Talk to me, girlfriend. What did you find out about the guys?"

"Well, hello, and how are you too?" Amy asked.

"Sorry, but I'm really stressed right now."

"Okay, I did my best Nancy Drew, and I didn't find out much, but maybe it will help. I found a few tidbits in the local newspaper archives from your neck of the woods. It seems our boy Chase has quite an imagination."

"How so?"

"The first info on him I found was a story from when he was sixteen years old. It described how a local boy, our own Chase Graves, claimed to have spotted a Sasquatch on a camping trip. He said they were attacked by the thing, and the local rednecks got a posse together, and one of them ended up falling off a bank and breaking his collar bone."

"That's pretty strange," Julianna said. *Wolfen!* "Did you find anything else?"

"There's a few stories in the same paper in some of the sports sections. Did you know he was his high school's quarterback?"

"Yeah, I heard that."

"Anyway, there's another story about him when he was in high school, and this one involves Shane too. The two of them were in a pretty intense fight. The teachers couldn't break them up, and the police were called. Can you imagine a paper writing that up? A high school fight? It was on a police blotter page."

"What about Shane?"

"Not much on him, except for the fight with Chase, and his mother's obituary. She was killed in the same way as your mom, person or persons unknown. But don't pretend with me, Jules. I know it's Chase who winds your clock. I'm not stupid, and he sure has the hots for you."

"Too much so."

"He's too much of a man you mean. Chase this, and Chase that. It's all I heard for weeks after you met him, then as soon as the guy shows an interest in you, you blow him off. Afraid he might get to you? Wow, I thought I had a fear of commitment, but you…"

"Stop, Amy, please. Did the paper say why they were fighting?"

"No, even that Podunk paper wouldn't give that much ink to a story like that. But…are you ready for this? I looked up his graduating class, and got the phone number for some kids he went to school with. I hit pay dirt with one girl. She remembered the fight. She said it was terrible, but like a car wreck where you can't wrench your eyes away, you know, even if someone was hurt."

"Did she say what they were fighting about?"

"She said that Chase accused Shane of attacking his brother. Chase was kicking his ass when the cops showed up and pulled him off."

"Chase has a brother? I didn't know that."

"Yeah, twins no less! Guess their parents liked that cutesy shit, giving twins similar names. Hopefully, they didn't make them wear the same outfits too. Chase and Jase." She laughed.

*Jase!* The same name her sister said. The name Chase said in the hardware store parking lot.

# Chapter Eighteen

Julianna hung up and stared at the phone. What was Chase's deal? Was his brother here too? Could he have been the one who tried to seduce Lorelei? It killed her not to know. In fact, not knowing could kill them both! When she heard Lorelei stirring inside, she knew it was now or never. She pressed the number saved on her favorites.

"Julianna?" Chase answered.

"I have something that I think belongs to you, Chase."

"Besides my heart?"

"Actually, it's a nice shiny silver compass. The really interesting thing, though, is where I found it. Care to guess where that was?" The phone went silent, and she checked the bars to make sure the call didn't drop.

"Chase, are you still there?"

"I think it's time we have a talk," he said.

"I think maybe that's a good idea too. Do you know the Mexican restaurant?"

"I do. Parking lot in a half hour?"

"I'll be there."

Julianna stuck her head inside the cabin door.

"Lorelei, I'm going to town. One of the snares needs repair, and I need more rope."

"Cool, I'll come with you. Give me a couple minutes."

Lor couldn't know, and she didn't want to put her in more danger than she already was.

"Next time, I promise. They close early today, and I need to get there before then, and besides, you need to rest. I'll be back soon."

She lifted Xena from her lap, put her in the house, and the car was in reverse before Lorelei could protest. Julianna wasn't scared, but she'd picked a well-lit and very public place to meet, just in case. She didn't know a more happening place than Jose's on a Friday night.

The car lights picked up Chase's truck parked near the entrance. She pulled in beside him, and he jumped out to open her door.

"Hungry? Want to have a bite to eat while we talk?"

She put her arms around him, then stretched out on tiptoe and kissed him on the cheek. He hugged her, and their lips came together. Julianna gave Chase's upper lip a gentle nibble, and then smiled and pulled away.

"What was that for? Tell me so I can do it every day for the rest of my life." He grinned at her.

"I'm sorry. That was supposed to be an apology for the way I treated you over some misunderstandings, but don't make it more than that. That's all it was. We need to talk. It was Jase with my sister, wasn't it?"

"Yes, my brother Jase, but he didn't know…"

"Let's get in your truck." She pulled the knife from its sheath as she climbed in. When Chase got in the driver's seat, she pointed it at him.

His eyes widened. "What's that for?"

"Depends on your answers. It's plated with silver. Why were you sneaking around in our woods?"

"I was keeping an eye on the two of you, making sure you were safe."

"Keeping an eye on us I believe, but which was it? Were you being a peeping Tom, or were you scouting the house before you attacked us?"

"What? Neither one, I –"

"I thought you lied to me before, and I didn't want any more to do with you. Don't lie to me now, Chase." Julianna fixed her eyes on his.

"I have never lied to you, Julianna. I won't start now. Definitely not now, I need you to trust me."

"Are you a werewolf?" She raised the knife toward his throat.

"Hey, go easy with that, okay? It's what I wanted to talk to you about."

Julianna withdrew the knife, but only a little. "I'm listening."

"Yes, I mean no. I kind of was, but I'm not now. I was like Lorelei. It's a long story."

"I don't have anywhere else to be, do you?"

"Short version then. When I was sixteen, my brother and I went camping on the South Branch River. We packed up our gear into our canoe, and floated off, just as we had a dozen times before. The fish were biting, and the river pushed us along with little effort on our part. It was beautiful. Before dusk, we were further downstream than usual, and we set up camp in a new spot. I put up the tent, and Jase walked off in the woods to collect some dry firewood. It was a clear evening, the stars covered the sky, and the moon was so full, it looked pregnant.

"I remember thinking Jase would be back soon before I fell asleep. I woke up shivering, and pissed off at Jase. He should have had the fire blazing by then.

I heard a dog growling in the woods, and I yelled for Jase. When he didn't answer, I figured he was trying to scare me, but then I remembered Dad warning us about a pack of feral dogs roaming in the area. I didn't want to take any chances, so I dug through Jase's backpack. He always carried a little .22-caliber pistol loaded with hollow points and snake shot. I held the gun in one hand, my flashlight in the other and went into the woods to investigate.

"About fifty yards in, I heard a whimper, and I turned my light towards the sound. Your father is the only one who ever believed me about what happened next, Julianna."

"What? You knew my father?"

"Yes, a long time ago, but that's another part of the story. Let me finish. There was a clearing, and my brother was on the ground. Two huge hairy…things were leaning over him, growling, and snapping. I didn't consider the fact that the first round in the pistol was the snake shot, and would just piss them off. I really didn't think at all. I just started shooting, and fur flew on the biggest one's forehead. They threw their heads in the air, and let out this shrill howl, the thought of which still sends shivers up and down my spine. Then they charged. The smaller one clawed my arm, slapped me to the ground, and bit off a chunk off my upper lip." He nodded. "Yup, that's why I have the moustache. My brother grew one then too, whether to fool people about which one of us was which, or from some weird sympathy for me, I'm not sure. Anyway, I was on the ground trying to keep this thing off me, when the wolves perked up their ears at something I couldn't hear and fled into the woods. We followed their retreat by the sounds of the branches and saplings snapping. When we heard the hounds on their trail, Jase and I hurried back to our camp.

"I bandaged the bite on my brother's neck, and started wrapping the cut on my arm when the men and their dogs overran our camp. They had a lot of questions, and we answered as best we could, but they provided no answers to any of *our* questions. They examined our wounds, and listened carefully to our story about being attacked by Big Foot beasts, somehow managing to do so without laughing at us. I guess they could see we were pretty spooked by something."

"Maybe they knew it was werewolves that attacked you."

"Maybe so, but if they did, they didn't share that. And if they did, why did they let us go? They had to know what would happen to us, what we would become. But they told us to see a doctor when we got back home, then they turned the hounds loose on the trail again and took off."

"You said you're like Lorelei? You'd have me believe you're a virgin, after all the women I've seen you with? And that you aren't a full wolf?"

"I know you don't trust me, and I can understand that, but you know being an Initiate only restricts one thing… I guess the Bill Clinton definition of sex has some merit in my situation."

"This goes beyond trust, Chase. This is my life and Lorelei's! Don't forget, until only a few minutes ago, I thought you were a lying, arrogant, womanizing, murderous werewolf with a racist sexual agenda."

"Wow, you had a rather high opinion of me! I know I'm asking for a lot on faith, huh?"

Julianna stared into his eyes as if she were waiting for something, some sign that might prove his honesty – or deceit.

"Was it you? Did you save us from the wolves the night our mother was killed?"

Chase looked away from her intense gaze. "Yes, not that you'll believe me."

"I want to believe you. In fact, I think I do, but there's only way to know for sure." She unbuttoned her blouse and pulled it open. The cool night air tickled her naked breasts, and she dropped the knife and straddled his lap. "If you are what you say you are, prove it."

# Chapter Nineteen

Chase felt his jaw drop. Julianna's breasts were full and firm, and his hands ached to touch them, to cup the perfect globes, feel their weight, and let his fingers and lips trail to her engorged nipples. The sight was even better than his frequent fantasies imagined it.

"Wait, Julianna, I don't think you understood me. I said I *was* like –"

She leaned forward and kissed him, teasing his lips with her tongue. His body rebelled against him as his desire threatened to rip him in two. *No, he couldn't take her like this, not with another misunderstanding between them.*

"Ahh," he sighed when she moved, grinding her ass on his crotch. "Wait, I need to tell you…"

She fumbled at his belt.

"We have to get out of this damn parking lot," Julianna said. "Any ideas?"

"Follow me."

Julianna buttoned her blouse and they climbed out of the truck. Chase took her hand and led her to a shed in back of the restaurant. He pulled a key from his pocket, opened the padlocked door, and switched on a light before they entered.

"How convenient – and romantic." Chase noticed her gaze sweep the interior. Shelves with half-completed carvings lined the walls, and wood chips and sawdust covered a large wooden workbench. In the shadows of the far corner stood a tattered couch and a beat-up coffee table on which sat a small TV.

"Jose comes here to get away from the restaurant. He dabbles in wood carving, and I bring him chunks of basswood sometimes. It's safe and private, but no, not exactly romantic." He shrugged and locked the door from the inside.

"So, where were we?" Julianna asked. "What is it exactly that you can, or can't, do with me?"

Chase turned back toward her. Her blouse was again open, exposing her breasts. She unsnapped her jeans, and allowed them to fall to her ankles. She stepped out of them, and tossed them on the workbench. She held her arms wide, raising her breasts, begging for his attention.

"Now then, show me you can't have sex with me, wolf-man."

"That's what I am trying to tell you, Julianna. Actually, I'm sure I can, and God, do I want to." He smiled, and quickly unbuttoned his shirt.

She pulled her own shirt closed, and grabbed her pants, "You lied to me? You are a full Wolfen? Stay away from me, Chase!" She fumbled in her pants pockets as Chase took off his shirt and dropped it to the floor.

"Looking for this?" He offered her the knife, handle first. "Sorry, I was getting nervous with that thing pointed at me."

She took the knife and glanced at the front of his jeans. "I can relate."

"I said I was like Lorelei, and I was, but I found the wolf that infected me. I killed him, Julianna. The moon's pull is minimal on me now, and there's no physical change at all. Maybe my sense of smell is still better than most people's, but that's it."

Chase held his arms over his head, and his biceps swelled. "Look for yourself, you'll see there are no lingering signs of the change. Look, please, I need you to trust me."

"I'm locked in a carving shed, nobody knows I'm here with a possible werewolf, who just happens to be half-naked. Let's just say trust isn't easy under the circumstances."

"I didn't force you here, Julianna. I would never. And I won't force you to stay."

"Hell no, you won't! If you're a wolf, you could bite me, or . . . shit! I don't even know what happens to the human form of a Wolfen when they get off. You could snap my neck! I think I'll just trust my knife for now." She pointed it at him, then the door. "Let me out."

"Please wait." Chase knew if she walked out, she'd never look back. He placed his wrists in the sling used for lifting large pieces of wood, pulled it tight, and nodded at the pull rope.

"You can find out for yourself, Julianna, because I do trust you. You know if I was Wolfen, I'd display the signs by now, this close to the full moon. I'll be at your mercy in this thing. Or you can leave and keep wondering about me forever. If that's what you choose, the keys are there on the chair."

Julianna gave the rope a tug, and Chase's arms shot up in the air. He took a deep breath, and his chest muscles expanded. She pulled again, and his legs straightened, and his arms were pulled taut above him.

"Easy, Julianna."

She walked around him in a slow lazy circle, stopping behind him.

"See, I told you. No changes."

She pulled off his cap and lifted his hair.

"Your ears look normal enough." She stepped to his front, and with the blunt edge of the cold blade, pushed open his lips to look into his mouth.

"Smile, I want to see your teeth."

He opened his mouth."

"So far, so good."

He closed his eyes, feeling the back of the knife slide over his arms and across his chest, then it left his skin.

"Julianna?" His eyes popped open, but he didn't see her.

"How much do you trust *me*, Wolf-man?" she said from behind him."

"Haven't I proven it?"

"I'll try to trust you too then." She stood on the chair and released his wrists from the rope.

He pulled her into his arms. A desire so long denied could no longer be repressed, and they succumbed to passion, each lover spurring on the other as the fever of lust consumed them.

In the post-orgasmic denouement, they held each other, quietly cuddling on the couch before Julianna broke the silence.

"Maybe there's no physical wolf changes now, Chase, but I swear you were growling. Is that a holdover? Is there anything else I should know about?"

"Nothing… nothing important anyway."

"Are you actually blushing after what we just did? You promised me – no lies."

"Well, since I've been free of the curse, I still feel stronger, I heal faster and my senses are keener. I don't know if that will wear off over time or not."

"And? What else?" Julianna stared at him, and he knew she wouldn't let him off the hook so easily.

"If you really must know, I get crazy horny throughout the whole moon cycle. I can hardly control it, and…"

Julianna placed a finger over his lips and nibbled on his ear lobe.

"Prove it," she whispered.

# Chapter Twenty

The man slammed his vehicle's door and limped along the ridge trail. The last hundred yards to the family's shack was by foot only. Better security that way, and security was important to all creatures of the night. As he approached the hovel, he smiled, wondering what the college kids would think of his abode. Some nice clothes and a haughty attitude were enough to convince them of a small fortune waiting for him after graduation. They were inferior and gullible creatures.

It had been a long day, and the added exertions of the night nearly did him in. He welcomed the few hours of sleep waiting for him inside. Only one lamp was lit in the small room that served as their living room and dining room. *Good, the old man is either out, or already in bed.* He slipped in the front door and bent down to pull off his boots. When he stood back up, he saw his optimism wasn't warranted.

"Where the hell you been, boy?" the older man demanded, his bourbon-laced breath striking at the same moment as the words.

"You know damn well –" He saw the old man poised to strike, and he threw up his arm to deflect it, but he was too slow. The older man's fist crashed down on the back of his head, and the impact drove him to his knees.

"Don't smart-ass me, you fucking puppy! I'm still the Alpha, and always will be as long as you are the only contender. Are you're thinking of challenging me?"

The younger man shook his head and remained on the floor. He was every bit as large as his older tormentor, but the memories from years of beatings stayed his hand.

"As I thought. You aren't ready to be a man, much less a Wolfen. So you spent another night hiding in the bushes playing with yourself, and watching the pretty girls play. Didn't you?"

"I've done more than watch. I was with Julianna!"

"I know better. You only got close to getting in her britches because you slipped some shit in her wine. Yeah, that's right, you're not the only one who owns a pair of binoculars. You need to be more aggressive, boy. Haven't I taught you how to deal with females? They're two little women, and you're a Wolfen, for God's sake."

"I'm winning their trust. They will be good assets to the pack if we handle them right."

"You handle whatever you want. I don't care if you handle that little prick of yours until it turns black and blue, but know this. If those two girls aren't served up to the pack on a platter and turned during the next moon, I'll rip your chicken shit heart out myself. We lost too many brothers over them, and the pack is keeping an eye on you. I won't be made a fool of."

The grey-haired man swung his booted foot, and it connected with the young man's midsection.

"Fuck!" he yelled, and doubled over. The next blow connected with his knee.

He crawled to his room as his father sat in his recliner and poured more bourbon into his glass. "I've had enough of his crap, and it's almost my time," he mumbled to himself. It was past time for a change. The old man would be proud of him soon enough. He planned a special treat for the pack, and when both of the women were his, the pack would fall in line and follow his lead.

His brother was no longer a concern and could no longer be the heir apparent, and that fueled the old man's anger. The old man chose his brother over him long before either of them reached puberty, but fate decided the sequence of their birth, not him. Nor was he responsible for his brother losing his ability to breed. One of the sisters' silver bullets took care of that, and a eunuch would never be the pack's Alpha.

Yes, he would finally make the old bastard proud, and he'd wrench the leadership of the pack from him at the same time. The old dog would pay for the years of beatings, the years of condescension. His father must die.

# Chapter Twenty-One

Julianna sped along the curving mountain roads in a hurry to get back home. It was a new moon, so there were no worries about werewolves, and Lorelei managed her post-full moon cycle well. Except for the horniness, she thought with a smile. But Lorelei might still need her, and she felt negligent for having left her alone for so long.

Lorelei sat on the porch with a half glass of wine when Julianna pulled in the drive. Xena lifted her head from the floorboards, but didn't run over to her mistress as usual. She laid her head down again, and curled back up to sleep.

Julianna pointed at the wine glass. "Not turning into an alchy are you, Sis?"

Lorelei sniffed the air. "You're not turning into a slut are you, Jules? I can smell the sex on you from here. Crap, it's hard enough keeping my hormones in check, couldn't you at least take a shower before you come home? And where's the rope you went to town for?"

Julianna's eyes flashed. "I guess we both have our vices."

Lorelei stood and turned toward the cabin door.

"Wait, Lorelei. I'm sorry I lied to you. I was afraid things wouldn't turn out well tonight. I thought I might be facing a werewolf."

"But he ended up being the warm fuzzy kind of wolf, a werewolf with a soul like in the movies, so you decided to screw his brains out instead."

"No, well, yes and no. He's not a werewolf, but he was in the same situation as you are. He calls it being an Initiate. Anyone who has never fully changed. He and his brother, Jase – your beau from the river, remember him?

They were attacked as teenagers. Chase said they want to help us, and he knew Dad, and he was here the night Mom was killed, and God, I don't know why, but I didn't even think to ask. I think he was the one who brought us home that night."

"You didn't think to ask? There must have been a lot on your mind."

"Okay, enough. I messed up, and yes, I got laid. I feel bad for lying to you, and even worse for leaving you alone when you weren't feeling well, but let's move past it. Deal?"

Lorelei stared at the stars and didn't respond for a moment. "I don't care about that. You shouldn't have gone alone. You could have been hurt. That's what sisters are for, what family is for, to be there for each other. "

Julianna knew how her sister felt. Lorelei deserved better treatment, a better sister, and a better protector. But she'd had no choice. She couldn't have chanced taking Lorelei with her, but she still owed her the truth. It was no less than Julianna expected, no, demanded, from her own friends. Instead, she'd left Lorelei to fend for herself, wondering with each passing moment if her sister was dead on the side of the road somewhere. She retreated into the cabin, and returned with her own glass of wine, and the bottle. She bent over her sister, topped off her glass, and kissed the top of her head.

"I'm really sorry, Lor. It won't happen again. Friends?"

Lorelei looked up, smiled, and hooked Julianna's outstretched pinky finger with her own.

"No, better than friends. We're sisters."

"So, I have a picnic date set up for tomorrow," Julianna said to change the subject.

"Cool, Jules. I hope you have fun. He must be a pretty special somebody for you to have a round two."

"We, Lorelei. You're coming along too. I hope we have fun."

"No way, I'm not going to be the third wheel. You just go and enjoy yourself."

"Jase will be disappointed."

"Jase?"

"Yeah, you know, the guy groping you down by the river? He's Chase's twin brother, and a little old for you, but that didn't seem to bother you the other day."

"Can't." Lorelei pointed to her extended teeth.

"His werewolf is still out there. He's the same way you are. He was bitten as a child."

"Geez, is there anyone from around here not affected by werewolves? They should change the nickname of West Virginia to 'The Werewolf State.' Unbelievable." She nodded. "Okay, I might as well take part in a picnic of my peers. So how did Chase know our Dad?"

"I don't know, but he'll fill us in tomorrow."

"You didn't have time to ask about much, did you?" Lorelei smirked.

"Don't start that again. I said I was sorry."

"How was he?" Lorelei asked.

"You were ten when Dad died. You remember him. He was a great father." Julianna tried to hide her grin.

"Ha-ha, smart-ass, you know exactly who I meant, but just in case he literally screwed your brains out… this Chase guy, was he any good?"

"Incredible, Lor, just incredible."

"Really? That good, huh?"

Except for her family, Chase was the first person she'd ever shared her secret with. The first guy she could be totally honest about this huge part of her life. The first one who understood. She thought of his smile, and the caring look in his eyes as he made love to her.

"Hello? Earth to Jules, do you read me, over?"

"Good enough that he scares me," Julianna said. "How's that?"

"Do you trust him?"

"Almost."

# Chapter Twenty-Two

Julianna stared at the old carving shed and smiled as Chase's truck pulled up beside them.

"Lunch is all packed. Where are we going?" she asked.

"Follow us. I think you'll like the spot we picked out. It has a great overlook with a beautiful view of South Mountain and the river."

The drive was short, and the location looked too familiar to Julianna.

"What's wrong, Jules?"

"Oh shit, it looks a lot different in the daylight, but I think I've been here before," she said softly.

"What did you say?" Lorelei asked.

Julianna didn't answer and stepped from the car. She met the men halfway, and extended her hand to Jase in greeting.

"Hi Jase. I'm Julianna, and I believe you've met my sister, Lorelei?"

"Yeah, I've met you too." He rubbed behind his ear. "You didn't bring that damn stick, did you?"

"No, I promise, no weapons. I'm so sorry, Jase."

He laughed. "No harm done. I sometimes have that effect on the ladies, but Chase was tickled to death. He usually takes the beat-downs because of something I've done."

"Chase, this is my sister, Lorelei."

Chase stuck out his hand, but Lorelei pulled him in for a hug. When they parted, Lorelei's smile split her face. *Not so worried about showing those teeth now*, Julianna thought.

"It's a pleasure to meet you under different circumstances, Julianna, and it's good to be formally introduced, Lorelei," Jase said.

"And this is poor little neglected Xena." Chase picked her up, and scratched the pup behind the ears.

Julianna looked at Chase, then at Jase. "How did even your mother tell you two apart?"

"It's easy," Jase said. "I'm the good-looking one! Seriously though, mine is a whole lot bigger than Chase's. Here, I'll show you."

The sisters looked at each other as Jase unsnapped his pants. Lorelei arched one eyebrow, and her lips parted as she openly stared. Jase pulled out his tucked T- shirt and lifted it over his head.

"See?" He pointed to a long scar stretching from his left shoulder to the center of his well-developed pectoral muscles. "Yup, my scar is a lot bigger than those little scratches that Chase carries, but oh… what did you girls think I meant?"

"That's not the first time he's used that line," Chase said, "but to make it easier on everyone growing up, and so I wouldn't get blamed for all of Jase's crap, I parted my hair on the left, and he parted his on the right. It's been easier for everyone since I grew the moustache and the grey parts came in."

Jase laughed. "Dad could always tell the difference. Chase is his favorite, first born by a few minutes, don't ya know."

"Chase, can I talk to you?" Julianna pulled him to the back of her car.

"Anything wrong?"

"Does that little trail over there lead to the overlook?" She continued when he nodded, "I'm not sure how to, or even if I should tell you this, but I've been here with someone before."

"Shane? Of course it would have to be Shane." His eyes turned as dark as tar when he faced her.

"We're being honest with each other, right? Would you rather I didn't tell you?"

"I can't stand the thought of you being with him, but only Shane would bring a guy's girl to that same guy's family farm."

"Well, I didn't know it was your family's land, Chase, and I'm sorry for that, but *a guy's girl*? Your girl, Chase?"

"Well, after last night, I ..."

"Look, last night was great, but I'm not anybody's *girl*. I like you a bunch, maybe too much, but I've made no promises to you or anyone, understand?"

"I understand you've been hurt a lot, Julianna, but you can trust me. Want to talk about it?"

Julianna walked away and grabbed the basket of food from her back seat.

"Maybe someday then," he said to her back.

"What's up with those two?" Lorelei asked Jase as Julianna, followed by Chase, swept past them toward the trail. "Hmm, I guess we missed something."

"Not an auspicious beginning. Shall we join them?"

When Jase and Lorelei reached the overlook clearing, the blankets were spread on the ground and Julianna was laying out the plates. Chase was sitting on his cooler, beer in hand, staring out over the river.

"This is beautiful, Jase. So peaceful and quiet, and what a view! Come here, look. There's an otter playing in the river! I bet you have to constantly chase off the teenagers making out up here! I can't believe I've never heard about it before."

Jase put his hands on her waist. "I've got you if you want a better look." She leaned forward slowly, angling out over the precipice.

"Hold on to me, Jase. You better not let go!"

"Never!"

"Oh, look. There's a woman's blouse hung up in the branches down there. I'll bet she got laid right here." Lorelei laughed. "I told you it must be a great make-out spot!"

Julianna sat on the blanket and put her head in her hands. *Shut up, Lorelei. Please just shut the hell up!*

"Hey Jules, come look at this. Some girl got lucky, and she had a blouse exactly like yours!" Lorelei turned her head as Julianna approached, and Jase pulled her upright.

"Enough about the blouse!" Julianna whispered in her sister's ear and returned to the blankets.

"Let's eat," Jase said. "We have a lot to talk about."

They lounged on the blankets and dug into the fried chicken and potato salad the women had brought.

"Okay, so 'fess up. Who saved our butts the other night? Nice butts I know, but still…" Lorelei licked her finger, touched it to one firm rounded cheek, made a sizzling sound, and laughed.

"Wow, you sure blush easily," she said to Chase.

Julianna looked at him, and their eyes met. Neither was able to bite back the sudden laugh.

"Guess we missed something again, Jase." Lorelei reached over to take the beer from Chase's hand. She guzzled it down and gave him back the empty can. "It was you, wasn't it?"

Chase got up, went to the cooler for a fresh beer, and returned to the blanket. "Yeah, it was me."

"Don't think I didn't appreciate what you did, but did you drug me that night? Were you trying to maintain your secret super hero identity or something? I wouldn't have said anything – even if I could see under your hoodie."

"Obviously I didn't want the Wolfen to recognize me, but it was the antidote to the potion that I gave you. It would seem that it's an amazing sleep aid too."

"How did you know about the potion or the antidote?"

"Seeing you out during the full moon. I figured you must have found something that worked in Helena's notes. The antidote part was easy – you left the book open on the table beside two clearly labeled bottles."

"Well, we owe you big time." Lorelei put her arms around him, kissed his cheek, then turned and planted one on Jase's mouth. "Thank you, my heroes!"

"You don't owe me anything, but even if you did, it's paid in full." Chase met Julianna's eye. She cleared her throat and looked down at the blanket, not able to prevent the amused smile on her face.

Jase frowned. "Hey Lorelei, you ever get the feeling you're the only one in the crowd who doesn't get the joke?"

## Chapter Twenty-Three

"What in hell possessed the two of you to go after the pack during the Spring Gathering anyway?" Jase shook his head. "I couldn't believe it when Chase told me you went hunting."

"What's the Spring Gathering?" Lorelei asked.

"Your parents didn't tell you? The local packs get together four times a year at each change of the season. The Spring Gathering was held here this year, and it runs for about a week. Lucky for all of us, you only met up with a small hunting party, or it would have gotten pretty hairy, no pun intended."

"So Chase, tell us how you knew our father, and get us up to speed on what we're up against," Julianna said around a mouthful of chicken.

"I guess the beginning is as good a place to start as any. After Jase and I were attacked, we started noticing the changes in ourselves. We bulked up some sure, but that seemed normal enough. We were teenagers after all, but we began getting into trouble at school, fights, that sort of thing, but we were totally unprepared for the next full moon."

"We attacked our own father," Jase said.

Chase nodded and continued. "Thank God we didn't bite him or anything, just threw him around some. We didn't even remember it the next day, and we thought Dad was off his rocker when he started dragging us to church for chats with Reverend Jim about our aggressive natures. He even hauled us in to Ramsey to talk with some shrink. The next full moon though, we changed again. We were in the basement playing foosball, and Dad ran upstairs and locked the door behind him. The next night he took us to see an old Indian man who was having a sweat in the lodge at his house. He told Dad he'd try to help us."

"An old Indian man. Our father?" Lorelei asked.

"Yeah, and no harm meant, but we thought he was a crazy old coot at first, until the next full moon changed us again." Jase said.

"So he told us what we were, and what he was too. He asked about our change, showed us his teeth, and looked at ours. He said we were cursed, but it was up to us whether we gave our souls over to our inner beast or not. He told us what to expect and when, and how important virginity was in staving off the full effect of the disease. That and not tasting the blood of your first Wolfen kill. Unlucky for Jase, he got lucky shortly after he was bitten. All of that animal magnetism of his I guess."

Julianna jumped up from her seat on the blanket. "Wait a minute! Jase, you aren't still an Initiate? You're a full wolf?"

"Yes, but don't look at me like that. I'd never hurt you or Lorelei. We are sworn to protect you, and Chase keeps me under lock and key when I'm transformed."

"What do you mean you're sworn to protect us?"

Chase held up his hands. "I'll get to that—patience. So, our Dad put in a steel door to replace the wooden one we'd chewed up, and he locked us in the basement during the next full moon. When we changed again, it was obvious your father was right about us, and we went to see him again. I'm not sure why he trusted us, but Thane promised to tell us everything if we would swear to protect his three girls: his wife and two daughters. He gave me his pocket watch to remind me of the moon's pull and of our promise."

"You left the watch with our mother... that night," Julianna said.

"Yes. I failed Thane, and Helena paid the price, but we won't fail again!"

"Not your fault, brother. Every time the sisters needed us most, during the full moon, I was out of commission, caged up with the change. This mind meld thing we have gets even worse after you're full Wolfen, and there is longer range reception too. I had to keep a lot of distance between myself and Lorelei. You've had to do it all alone. I didn't even recognize them at the river the other day. My binoculars are crap for clarity." Jase said, and lowered his eyes.

"Binoculars, really?" Lorelei laughed.

Jase looked at her with raised eyebrows. "Yes, why?"

Lorelei shook her head and glanced at Julianna.

"We had a Peeping Tom spying on us up on the ridge when we were swimming. My first day home. Was that you, Jase?" Julianna asked.

"No, I swear. Chase and I didn't even get here from college until a day or so later. Chase had another exam and didn't trust me to come alone I guess. I think you saw me at the restaurant right after we got here. Sorry for that too, by the way."

"Well, brother, if you're apologizing, how about why you didn't bother to mention your encounter at the river, or about how Julianna kicked your butt."

"Hey, she's like a woman possessed when she gets her hackles up. I'll make no excuses for that. As to the other, hell, that's as much your fault as mine. You also failed to mention to me that you'd been seeing Julianna."

"Okay, okay, I guess we both screwed up, and you haven't seen them since college started, Jase. They've changed some."

"Well, you were a little occupied defending yourself from a crazy woman," Julianna added, smiling at Jase. "But if you boys are done bickering, I'd like to hear the rest of the story."

"Right. Anyway," Chase continued, "shortly after you were born, Julianna, your father was turned by the Alpha wolf – Malcolm. Thane said it was because he was getting too close to the pack, learning their secrets, suspecting who the Wolfen were in the community."

"At first, he embraced the change, said he loved the freedom and the power, but he was never truly accepted by the pack because he didn't prey on humans. Eventually, Malcolm grew more and more bloodthirsty, and one night, he led the pack on a hunting trip, more like a rampage really, and they killed four young campers and some kids up on Ice Mountain. Your father had enough. He tried to sway the pack against their leader, against murder, but Malcolm found out. On the weekend before the full moon, he and two of his boys crept up to your cabin to confront your old man. Thane was gone. He expected a confrontation during the full moon, but thought he was safe until then, and no Wolfen pack attacks their own member's families. But I guess Malcolm didn't hold with any of the old rules and traditions."

"So they bit our mother in retaliation when they didn't find Dad," Julianna finished for him.

"Bit?" Chase said, looked at Lorelei, then clamped his mouth closed. Julianna, her head tilted, was squinting at him. *Shit, why did I say anything? She didn't know!*

"What are you holding back, Chase?" Julianna asked.

"Sorry, I was spacing…thinking about our river trip. Umm…where was I? Oh yeah, after the attack on your family, your father started a secret war against the murderers in the pack, all the while trying to convince the others that human life was sacred. When we met up with him, he must have known it was just a matter of time before they got to him. Dozens of killers had fallen to your father's blade and traps over the years prior, and many others fled the area to start new packs, away from

Malcolm's influence. They had enough of Malcolm's reign too. The rest of Malcolm's pack caught up with your Dad one night during his change. He was betrayed. You know the rest."

"That's the year Mom made me miss a whole year of school," Lorelei said. "She lost touch… with everything… after we lost Dad. You've been watching us ever since?"

"It really hasn't been all that bad of a duty, and it's gotten a whole lot better now that we dropped the 'protect from afar' method," Jase answered with his wolfish smile and lightly rubbed her thigh. Lorelei slapped him on the shoulder and looked to her sister, who was still staring at Chase.

"Would you take me for a walk, Jase?" Lorelei asked. "Show me around some?"

"Sure." She and Jase walked off, hand in hand.

"She thinks we need some time alone," Julianna said.

"Yes."

"What did you leave out, Chase? No lies."

He walked toward her, took her hands in his, and looked deeply into her eyes.

"It isn't something you need to know, Julianna, and it doesn't change anything."

"Tell me, Chase. I'll decide if it's important or not."

He looked away. "I'd rather not."

Julianna crossed her arms over her chest. "Too bad."

"Okay then. If I must. It was days before the full moon. The pack members were in human form. They didn't bite your mother, Julianna, they raped her."

"No, Chase, no!"

He caught her up in his arms when her knees buckled. He gently guided her to the observation rock, and her head fell to his shoulder.

"Oh my God, Mom, I'm so sorry… I didn't know, please forgive me!" she moaned, shaking her head.

Chase hugged her to his chest, ashamed that even at such a moment, she aroused his passions. He grew stiff at the mere touch of her. Her clean earthy scent – mayapple and honeysuckle, cedar, pine, and wild mint, all rolled into one overwhelmed his wolfish senses, even as his own eyes blurred, sharing the anguish of her soul.

"Chase, does that mean that Lorelei is …?"

"There's a good chance she's Malcolm's daughter. He was the Alpha." He held her until her trembling stopped.

# Chapter Twenty-Four

"What do you think those two are talking about, Jase?"

"I don't know, but something's been going on since we got out of the car. I hope they can work it out. Chase is really smitten with your sister."

"Smitten?" Lorelei laughed. "Poor Chase is smitten. It sounds like a condition or something." She pretended to hold up a microphone. "Chase Graves is reported in good condition today after being severely smitten. Tune in for Channel 3's special report at eleven—'How to keep your family safe from the Smits.'"

Jase chuckled. "I guess it is a condition. He always had a crush on her, but it's been worse since they went off to college."

"I think I'm sorry to hear that. Chase is a sweet guy, and Julianna isn't a big fan of commitment, you know."

"The same with Chase, so they're not really different in that way. What happened with Julianna? Chase thinks something bad happened to her that changed her when she was a teenager. He's been beating himself up over it for a lot of years…because he wasn't there for her."

Lorelei shrugged her shoulders. "If I had to guess, I'd say it was her senior year, and I'll bet you dollars to peanuts that it had something to do with a guy. But what brought you and Chase back home? Are the college girls not hot enough for you?"

"You were still too young to be of much interest to the pack when Julianna went to college, so we followed her, and when she came back…well, here we are. We would have come anyway, but this time Chase was on a mission."

"Why this time? What changed?"

"He said three special moons in a row spelled trouble, and he heard that the Wolfen were stirred up and seemed to be waiting for something. There was the full moon anniversary of Malcolm becoming the Alpha wolf, and then the moon during the Spring Gathering, of course, but it's the next one, the super moon, when the moon is the closest to us. That one has him really worried."

Lorelei shook her head. "You guys are really up on this stuff. Why haven't you tried to find the wolves that bit you?"

"Of course we tried. For years and years we tried. I should say that Chase did, because I wasn't much help there. Then over time, the full moon ordeal became such a regular part of our lives that our quest became less determined. It became our new normal."

"Chase started hunting again when you came back home this time?"

"Oh yeah. He was focused on killing the wolves that attacked us again, or die trying. He said if he had any chance of protecting the two of you, and any chance with Julianna, he needed to be free of the curse."

"I can understand that. I envy his success, and his new freedom. It must be like getting a new lease on life, a rebirth. So, the two of you have been spying on us since our father died, nine years ago. And now, Chase has the hots for my sister."

"Sure seems that way."

"What about you, Jase?" She pouted. "There's another Stone daughter, you know – one you seemed quite interested in the other day when you didn't know who I was. I'd like to think you might have developed some feelings for me that went beyond protection. Like Chase did for Julianna."

"You were just a girl when I left, remember? Now you're…"

Lorelei smiled, licked her upper lip, and he pulled her into his arms.

"Now I'm what?"

"Are you fishing for compliments? If so, I'm glad to oblige. You are nothing less than unbelievable, a head-turning fantasy goddess." Her breasts pressed against him, and he felt his immediate response.

"Can I trust you? You know I can't go all the way."

"You trusted me before." He kissed her deeply, then nibbled at her neck.

She pushed her palm against his chest and stepped back. "I was in a bad way that afternoon, a real horndog, or hornwolf, actually. Don't take this the wrong way, but trust had nothing to do with it."

"And now?"

"Ahh, I'm getting there, trying to trust you I mean."

"You should, at least today. I'm not sure the other day at the river was a good idea. It's probably a good thing that Julianna showed up—speaking for myself here."

"I thought the same thing, later that is, but don't tell her that!"

"No worries, I have an over-protective sibling too."

"I want to apologize for acting so slutty that day. The moon does a number on me, twists me up inside. It makes me someone else until it's all I can think about."

"The moon? Is that the only reason you were interested in me? You sure know how to hurt a guy."

Lorelei laughed. "Oh, are you the one fishing for compliments now? Well, you're the studliest wolf-man I've ever met. How's that? But I know you understand the moon's pull. Or do you? Is it easier after…"

"When you're no longer a virgin and are a full Wolfen? Is that what you are asking?"

"Yes."

"Remember, I was a teenager when first bitten. My hormones were already raging. And when the wolf's blood is peaking, I'm still chained up—just like you."

"Do you want to wander off the trail a bit? Find a nice grassy spot to relax – away from any prying eyes?

"No, not now anyway, Lorelei. They'll be wondering about us, and to be honest, I'm not sure I trust myself with you. God, you're sexy."

"Hmm, and you've never used that line before." She giggled, then her expression became serious. "Are you sure?"

"Please don't tempt me. I'm Wolfen, but I can't blame my poor self-control on the moon. Trust me when I say *not* to trust me just now."

# Chapter Twenty-Five

"Lorelei can't find out that Malcolm might be her father, Chase. Make sure Jase knows he can't mention it either."

"He knows how to keep a secret."

"I thought the grey-haired wolf I killed was Malcolm. He acted like the Alpha wolf. Shouldn't Lor be free of the curse now too?"

"Malcolm was wounded, but he's still very much alive. It takes a lot to kill an Alpha wolf, and to be honest, I don't know what will happen to Lorelei when he is killed. She's Wolfen by birth. Breaking her curse might be harder than it is for a person who only becomes Wolfen after they're bitten."

"So how did you do it? Did you just get lucky? Killing the wolf that attacked you, I mean."

"Yes, I was lucky. Lucky and determined, but the one who attacked my brother, as well as your mother's rapists, are still out there."

"We'll find them, Chase."

"Yes, it's time for it to end – chaining my brother up, hearing his pain, and hiding for three days every moon cycle. We've been careful, and we've taken good care of each other. Maybe that stopped us from ending this sooner, but it needs to stop now."

"I'm not complaining. I can't tell you how grateful we are for the help. But why now?"

He reached out and held her shoulders in his hands. "You, you're why. I had to free myself from the curse if I ever hoped to be more than your protector. I decided it was do or die time."

"Lorelei said pretty much the same thing."

"Who's talking about my beautiful goddess?" Jase said as he entered the clearing with Lorelei.

"We were just…" Julianna looked to Chase.

"Talking about ridding her of the curse, and you too. We need to find the wolf who bit her mother, and the one who infected you as well." Chase shot a warning glance at his brother.

"That won't be easy. We have no idea how many there are," Lorelei said.

"Our father tried, and look what it got him. We can't take them all out." Julianna pursed her lips. "But we have to do something."

Jase nodded. "You went against them at the worst possible time. Their numbers were inflated at the Spring Gathering. There won't be so many on the next full moon."

"And some aren't murderers," Chase said. "Your father knew that. Most of the Wolfen consider themselves cursed, as we do. Malcolm's family considers it a divine right and blessing."

"Is there any way to weed them out? A way to determine which ones are responsible?" Lorelei asked.

"I say we string ol' Shane up to a tree, and beat it out of him!" Jase swung an imaginary baseball bat.

"Good grief, what is it with you two and Shane?" Julianna said and shook her head. "Are you sure he has something to do with it? Please tell me that it's not still sour grapes because he beat Chase out as starting quarterback, or some other macho crap."

Jase frowned at her. "Beat him out? Is that what our old buddy Shane told you? Julianna, that never happened. Chase got suspended and kicked off the team because of that fight with Shane in high school. They decided he was at fault, said he was the aggressor, but Chase knew it was Shane's family who attacked us, and Shane got off scot-free."

"Shane's family? How do you know that?"

The brothers looked at each other, and Chase scratched the side of his head. “Julianna, we knew Malcolm was the leader of the attack on us. Remember I shot him? It left a grey streak of hair that wasn’t there before that night.”

Julianna spread her hands. “Okay, so?”

“You know Shane is Malcolm’s son, right?”

# Chapter Twenty-Six

Amy twisted the setting on her vibrator from "Yeah Baby" to "Buzz Saw," then all the way up to "Oh My God," and watched the little balls rotate faster and faster around the base of the shaft. At least the manufacturer had a sense of humor, she thought. That was more than she could say for the guy she just chased out of her bedroom. He reminded her of the neighbor's horny toy poodle back home, always humping on her shin when she sunbathed by their pool. Neither of them knew what they wanted, weren't sure how to catch it, or what to do with it if they did. She learned a valuable lesson though. Never pick up a guy at a cyber café!

She'd picked the guy up out of pity more than anything. Well, okay, who was she kidding? She needed the relief sex too, but he did nothing to scratch her itch. After one evening together, he started with some inane post-coital spiel about their future together. He asked her when she thought she could meet his parents for Christ's sake!

So she broke out her little toy to help things along, and the boy went old school on her. He didn't want to be with any woman he didn't satisfy. He didn't believe in toys, just what nature provided. Well, Ma Nature didn't provide you with much, buddy!

So in the course of ten minutes, she went from practically engaged to dumped and unsatisfied. Alone now, she stared at her wonder toy, sighed, and cranked it up to "Oh My God."

When she heard a thump at her front door, she thought maybe Poodle Boy had a change of heart. Maybe it wouldn't be a wasted night after all! She switched off the vibrator and set it on her nightstand. Then thought better of it, and switched it back on so he could hear it as soon as he walked in the door. Maybe it would get his motor running too.

She slipped on her sheer robe and hurried to the door. She looked through the peephole and saw the back of the man's head. It wasn't Poodle Boy, but oh crap, what did he want? She was so horny, she considered opening the door and throwing the moves on him.

She opened the door slightly, but left the chain on, and peered out.

"What are you doing here?"

"I was in the neighborhood and thought I'd stop by. Have you talked to Julianna yet?"

"Yes, I told her the truth about the other night if that's what you're worried about."

"Thank you. The truth shall set us free."

"Umm, okay."

"Can I come in? I want to talk to you about Julianna."

"Now's not good, I've got company, but we can get together soon and talk. Or give me a call. I've got to go now. Good night." Amy gently closed the door, and smiled at the sound of the vibrator working its way across the table in her bedroom. *Oh well, I guess it's just you and me tonight, old buddy.*

As she fastened the latch, the door rattled in its frame. She stood back. What the hell? Was the bastard trying to break in? A second blow splintered the door jamb, and Amy stood paralyzed with fear. Too late, she thought of her cellphone. The door crashed open.

"Bitch!" the man growled as he rushed in and grabbed her shoulders, digging in with his nails. Amy screamed as she struggled to break free from the powerful grip.

A blonde-haired woman with heavy makeup strolled in behind the man. "What do we have here?" she said. "Let her go so I can have a good look." The man released Amy and stepped aside. The woman's eyes moved up and down Amy's body. "Sweet."

"Help! Fire!" Amy yelled, and ran toward the kitchen. *The knives. Must get to the knives!* "Get the hell away from me. Are you fucking crazy?"

Just as she made it to the kitchen, the man hooked her robe with his claws. He drew her back toward him. She pulled away, and the robe ripped free in his hands. She stood naked facing them.

"What the hell do you want?" she cried, bending over and trying to cover herself with her arms.

"You." He smiled as he stood in the kitchen doorway, blocking her escape.

The blonde slid under his arms and stepped toward Amy. "Don't be shy, sweetie." She pulled Amy's arms away from her body. "Let us see you." The woman licked her lips. "Mmm, nice!"

She could handle the woman with a roundhouse to the face, but the knives were on the far counter; she couldn't reach them before the man reached her. She needed a distraction. *The clock!* She backed into the kitchen table and reached behind her for the cuckoo clock she'd tried to repair. Taking hold, she hurled it at the woman's head. The bitch ducked out of the way, but it was enough. Amy ran around the table, grabbing the broken clock pendulum on the way. Not daring to turn her back on her assailants, she held the pointed end of the wooden shaft in front of her as she backed up to the counter.

The man snarled and bared his teeth. *What's wrong with his teeth?* Hair sprouted on his face, and his…oh God, did his ears get longer?

"What the fuck are you?" she shouted. Her hand reached behind her to the knife drawer just as he sprang forward. Amy stabbed upward with the pendulum arm, and it penetrated his belly. He howled, bent over, and pulled the shaft out. His teeth make a popping sound as he stood erect.

The woman rushed past him, slammed Amy against the counter, trapping her left wrist painfully behind her against the counter edge. Amy's punches had no effect as the woman snatched a handful of hair and yanked Amy's head up and back, extending her neck.

"Thank you for your service. Goodbye, bitch." The woman's mouth opened, and her lips curled back. Amy screamed again at the horrifying sight, her mind not able to cope with what was happening. The woman's head pitched forward, and with one ravenous bite, ripped out Amy's throat.

The man heard the odd buzzing in the bedroom and went to investigate. He placed Amy spread eagled on the bed and shoved her toy down the bloody hole in her neck.

# Chapter Twenty-Seven

Julianna was shaken to her core with the news about Shane's parentage, but could she trust the twin brothers? Both her life and her sister's life hung in the balance. Obviously the brothers had an ulterior motive for casting doubt on Shane. Maybe Chase wanted to end the competition for her affections and her bed. Or worse, maybe they were the ones plotting against her family.

She had a good look at Chase at a time when he should have exhibited signs of the change. A real good look! Jase was full Wolfen and made no secret of the fact. Shane never gave any indication he even believed in such things as werewolves. What if the old fairytales were right? Could an experienced werewolf acquire new talents over time – like changing at will, or the ability to hide its true nature?

Julianna felt her sister's eyes on her as she sipped her morning coffee.

"You still don't trust them, do you?" Lorelei asked.

"Not a hundred percent. Should I? Do you?"

"What the hell was going on with the two of you yesterday? You were all happy to be meeting up with the guys and all of a sudden, you turned into the Ice Queen. Sorry, I should say the Ice Princess."

"Ha! You're so hysterical. Chase got all possessive with me, and I don't need that crap right now."

"Now or ever?"

"What?" Julianna asked, but Lorelei just sipped her coffee and smiled.

"By the way, that was my blouse on the cliff. Thanks so much for pointing it out."

Lorelei's laugh spewed coffee across the table. "Oh my God, I'm sorry, but that is so funny!"

Julianna grabbed a napkin to mop up the mess. "Maybe, but Chase didn't think so. It's like you said the other day, I didn't make any commitment to anyone. Did he think I was a virgin when he started with me?"

"I have a little sister to big sister tip for you, Jules. Guys are jealous critters, in case you haven't noticed. I know you aren't deceitful, but it wouldn't hurt if you left out some shit. They don't need to know everything. Really, what woman in her right mind tells a guy she likes that she's also seeing his worst enemy? That's she's been doing the naughty with him on his own farm. Duh!"

"I didn't…oh, never mind. One of them wants to kill us, Lor! Maybe both of them for all I know. Until I know for sure, what can I do? I can't let either of them know I'm suspicious, right?"

"Play the field with both of them if you want, choose between them when you're ready. My money's on Chase, but until you decide, just shut the hell up about it already."

"Yeah, I guess, but I can't just string them both along. I have to figure out how to make our enemy reveal himself, and before the full moon."

Julianna poured another cup of coffee. As she stepped past Lorelei, she pinched her sister's thigh.

"Ouch! What the hell was that for?"

Julianna took a deep breath to restrain her laughter. "I just realized I have some big sister to little sister advice for you. If you don't want your big sister to know what you were doing with a guy, you should wear a high-collar shirt to hide your hickey."

Lorelei's hand went to her neck as she blushed. "We didn't do anything. We just…"

Julianna's laugh brought her up short.

"Okay, Jules. I guess we're even now. But look, we know we can't kill them all. Even if their ranks were swollen last time, we still don't know how many there are, and we don't want to kill any innocents. So the problem is sorting them all out, and killing the two responsible for my and Jase's infection, right?"

"While I'm trying to maintain a normal relationship with two guys at the same time without raising their suspicions and, oh yeah, one of them is a murderer. That about sums it up." Julianna sighed.

"Do you still suspect Chase?"

"I don't know what to believe. Chase says that not only is Shane a wolf, but he was at the cabin that night. The night Mom died."

"How could he know that?"

"He claims he has a residual heightened sense of smell. That he knew it was Shane. But I don't know – the two of them obviously have an axe to grind with each other."

"Then we need to bait the wolves into revealing themselves. We want them dead, but they want us just as badly, and a Wolfen can't stand the thought of a virgin Initiate, especially during their transformation."

"No, absolutely not. We are not using you as bait again for a pack of werewolves! We can't use Mom's potion this time."

"Not me, you. I have a plan, Jules."

# Chapter Twenty-Eight

Julianna sat at the couch holding Xena tight and staring at her phone when Lorelei walked in from her shower.

"Okay, look. The makeup hides my little hickey, and…oh no, what's wrong, Jules?"

Julianna made no attempt to wipe away the tears flooding her face.

"Amy… Amy's dead, Lor. Some sick son of a bitch killed her, and I wasn't there to help her." She broke down into sobs.

Lorelei ran to her sister's side and wrapped her in her arms. "I'm so sorry, Jules. God, I'm so sorry."

"Jen called me. She and Deb wanted to meet up with Amy for lunch. They left her several messages but she never called them back, and you know Amy. She kept her cellphone permanently attached to her ear. They... they found her all torn up, and…" Julianna sucked in her breath.

"Jules, take your time."

"They found her like that yesterday. The cops have a guy in custody, somebody she was with at a café. When she left with him, it was the last time she was seen alive."

"Who is he?"

"Jen didn't know."

"Did she have any enemies, or any weirdoes hanging around her? Or stalkers maybe?"

"Lor, her throat was ripped out!"

"My God!"

"The police haven't released that information, but Jen and Deb were there, and they saw her. What do you think could do something like that?"

"They're going after our friends too, Jules."

"Amy was the best. I trusted her." A whimper escaped her as she recalled her doubt the morning after their last night together in the apartment. The apartment that was now a murder scene. Chase and Shane, it always came back to the two of them.

She sent them identical text messages. "Horrible news. Amy's been murdered! Leaving tomorrow. Please give me time to grieve."

She hit send, and the text replies and phone calls began within moments.

They either couldn't read, or they had no concern with how she felt. Or maybe they were concerned and wanted to help in any way they could – one of them anyway.

The answering machine on the cabin's landline clogged with messages, and she sent another text. "Please understand. Can't talk now. Funeral is Monday noon, St. Augustine's in Morganville, if you want to pay your respects."

The sisters packed for the trip. Julianna gave her sister a hug before locking herself into her room to grieve in private.

During the graveside service, Julianna had a sense of recent history repeating itself. Not quite déjà vu, but still. It didn't help that the two men she felt ambivalence toward were there again, standing behind her. She could feel them bumping into one another, jockeying for a position closer to her, until she turned and looked at them both with thunder in her eyes. At that moment, she could have ripped both of *their* throats out! Only then did they move off to give her space.

Julianna and Lorelei stepped forward at the end. They tossed a flower on Amy's casket, and Julianna hugged Amy's parents.

"Amy wasn't just my roommate, she was my dearest friend," she whispered in the mother's ear. "I am so sorry."

Chase and Shane split to opposite sides of the assembled mourners. Shane was closest, and she pulled him aside. He offered his condolences and hugged her.

"Sorry I've been out of touch, Shane. When things like this happen, it makes you remember to keep your friends close. I'd really like to have you over the cabin for dinner next Sunday. Early, say three or so? We always eat early on Sunday."

"I'd love to. Can I bring anything?"

"Maybe another bottle of that good homemade wine?"

"Can do. See you at three then."

Shane walked to his car and drove away. Julianna searched for Chase. She found him chatting with Jase and Lorelei.

"I was just telling the guys that we need to get together, a date." Lorelei said. "Chase said you two both really liked it at Jose's. Jase and I would like to double with you guys. That is, if it's okay with you, Julianna."

"It sounds like a great idea." Julianna stepped toward Chase, and he wrapped his arms around her. Jase and Lorelei wandered away holding hands.

"I don't know what to say. I know how horrible this must be for you," Chase said.

"It is, but it's left no further doubts for me. I have to avenge my mother, and Amy, and free Lorelei and Jase. Will you help me, Chase? Will you please help me?"

"That must have been hard for you, asking anyone for help, but I'll do anything for you."

*Please, oh please dear God, please, please don't let it be him.* Her head rested on his broad shoulder, and she sighed. Her eyes welled up with water, and she tried to hold it back, but a tear streaked down her cheek and fell to his suit.

# Chapter Twenty-Nine

"I like this place. It's so authentically Mexican, from the plastic cactus to the worn bricks painted on the walls, and of course, our hostess shaking her plastic maracas. Want to bet there's a 'Made in China' sticker on them?" Lorelei said with a grin.

"Yeah," Chase agreed. "I'll confess I definitely noticed the young woman shaking her maracas, but I don't think they're plastic. They looked pretty real to me."

"I had a pretty good look too, and I didn't spot any stickers on them. Maybe further investigation is required," Jase added.

Julianna and Lorelei rewarded their attempts at humor with punches to their arms.

"I haven't been in here since this was a McDonald's. Do you remember, Jules?" Lorelei asked.

"Yes, and it's not so different inside. The booths are laid out the same."

They claimed the far booth as their own and ordered drinks. Jose's was fairly quiet on a weekday evening, but that suited their needs.

"So, are we going to do this, take the fight to them?" Chase asked.

"We have to," Julianna said. "We don't know what we'll be facing, but what recourse do we have?"

"To be honest, I'm not very comfortable with either of you hunting."

Julianna clasped her hands together on the table and eyed Chase with a level gaze. "We have a plan, and it'll work. And you'll be a part of it." Her serious mien softened. "You'll get to play protector, Sir Chase, a role it seems you were born for. Lorelei and Jase will be together all day Sunday, giving them ample time to take care of each other before the full moon rises."

"Are you two all right with that?" Chase asked. "You might get in a bad way well before the transition, and have you ever seen a full transformation, Lorelei?"

"You're kidding, right?"

Chase laughed. "Oh yeah, silly question, huh? Okay, let's hear this plan of yours."

Julianna was about to respond when the waitress arrived with their drinks and to take their food orders. After they were alone again, Julianna resumed the discussion.

"So, Jase and Lorelei will be out of harm's way before we start the ball rolling – hours before the moonrise. They've wanted to turn Lorelei for years, especially during their wolf phase, but I don't think they pushed too hard as they thought she'd eventually be drawn to them anyway. I'll make Shane think the two of us are home alone, but when he comes to the cabin for dinner, Lorelei will be safely tucked away with Jase, and –"

"Whoa! What? Rewind to the part about Shane coming to dinner. What do you think you're doing? Setting yourself up as bait?" Chase gave her an incredulous look.

"Yes, that's exactly what I'm going to do, and it will work."

"No, I can't let you do that."

"You can't let me? You can't stop me, Chase. Look, I'm sorry. I know you mean well, and you have a knight in shining armor complex with me, and that's very sweet, but this is the best way to end this. It's something I need to do, have to do, and I want your help. So, are you in, or do I only have myself to count on?"

He sighed. "Let's hear the rest."

"There's not much left to tell. After a couple of hours, when Shane lets his guard down and gets comfortable, you'll come charging in, my brave knight. Together, we'll overpower him, and lock him in the basement room. When he changes at moonrise, assuming you're right about him, we'll kill him."

"You still don't trust me?"

"I don't think a little doubt is a bad thing when a man's life hangs in the balance."

"Fair enough, but Malcolm and Shane's brother Garret will still be out there for us to hunt."

"Those two and whoever's left from the Gathering."

"What's the plan for them?" Chase asked.

"A shit load of silver bullets, and a lot of determination."

"Let's hope that'll be enough."

Lorelei excused herself to go to the bathroom, and Julianna followed. "Come on, Sis, we're not going to be those women who have to go potty together now, are we?"

"I just wanted to tell you the other part of the plan, Lor."

"Other part? Didn't you just explain everything to the guys?"

"I added a small change. The plan, what I told them, assumes Shane is the killer, but you can't go to Jase's house that night. If Chase is the one, he might try to take you before he comes to the cabin. No, he can't know where you are. You'd be alone, at his mercy – the mercy of a full-blown wolf."

"It would be the same thing if I was on the throne at the cabin, plus they would smell me, and you wouldn't have a place to hold Shane." Lorelei said.

"Right, that's why we're not putting you there either."

"Where then?"

"Dad built the cell in the basement, but he also fixed up the root cellar in the backyard. It has solid concrete walls, and a steel door. Nothing will get in that we don't want to get in."

"You mean get in or get out."

"Yes, it's an intricate latch mechanism, but a rational human being can release it from the inside. While you're a wolf, cognitive abilities are reduced and you won't be able to figure it out. There are four chains embedded in the walls, just like in the cell. Dad was afraid Mom would turn after what happened, and he said he needed a place for a back-up. I checked it out this afternoon, and it looks good, but there aren't enough padlocks. We'll have to pick up another set."

"So, you think if Chase is the one, and we aren't at Jase's house, that he'll then go straight to the cabin?"

"Yes, like we planned, but if it is Chase, and not Shane, who changes and attacks, he gets a silver bullet to the chest."

"Could you do that, Jules?"

"I'm not sure." She stared at the sky, then rubbed her knuckles over her eyes. "Yes, I could. I'd have to."

"Why didn't Dad ever use the root cellar?"

"For the same reason there's a pair of steel-barred windows above the room in the basement instead of solid concrete. Dad said when the cellar door closed, it was pure torment for a wolf. He said smells didn't even get in there, and that a wolf who can't see, smell or feel the moon goes temporarily insane. The root cellar was intended for emergencies only."

"It sounds real appealing. Is that really what you want me to do, Julianna? Is there anybody you trust?"

"I trusted Amy, and I trust you. No, I don't want it, but it's the only absolutely safe place I can think of for you."

"Nobody is ever absolutely safe, least of all me, and some people can be trusted, Jules. I trust Jase."

"I know you do, but why? Think about it. Jase has been off of our radar. Hell, we weren't aware of his existence until recently. Chase is the only one who can verify his alibi of being chained up through all of the horrors. Jase might even be the wolf that killed our mother."

"He's not, Jules. I trust him."

"Okay, but does he trust you enough that you can talk him into going there on Sunday without telling Chase? He'll be chained to the wall in the cellar with you—so you'll be safe from him. But Chase is the wild card."

# Chapter Thirty

The man recovered quickly from his stomach wound. His skin scarred over, with only a little soreness remaining. The greatest benefit of being a Wolfen was the fast healing, and he had plenty of opportunities over the years to put it to the test. By the time the full moon rose again, nobody would know he was ever injured.

He considered it a shame about Amy. She died too soon. At least a half hour too soon. He could smell her aching need that night, but his companion was inexperienced and impatient, and killed her too quickly. That pissed him off. What fun Amy would have been to play with. It would have been so satisfying, so just, to take Julianna's best friend. Hell, she even supplied her own toys, and she was a screamer, too…what a waste.

What had the crazy bitch thought? That they were freaking vampires or something? Stabbing him with a chunk of wood? It was his good fortune that she didn't know to use silver. Lucky that Julianna hadn't trusted her roommate with all of her secrets, but it wasn't something a human could easily share with the blissfully ignorant masses. Not that he was excusing Julianna. Oh no, Amy's death was as much her doing as his, but he wouldn't share this kill, and his plans for the sisters were now carved in stone.

His mother warned him about his impatience. That was one of the reasons he'd opened her throat all those years ago. Funny, she was a strong Wolfen, but she didn't put up much of a struggle, even as he ripped through her jugular, and the hot blood gushed out her life. He blamed her murder on Thane Stone, of course. The old wolf proved to be a good scapegoat for him through his teenage years, and a worthy adversary. His brother only helped him with that kill but still got all the glory from their father.

He recalled Amy's expression when he wolf-morphed a bit for her "entertainment." Happy times. It drained a lot out of him to morph outside of the moon cycle, but he was getting better at it. Amy seemed impressed! One of the small talents he would hone as he took over as the Alpha wolf.

A fresh full moon, and a fresh start, waited for him only a few days away. His well thought out plot hadn't played out exactly as planned, but he could adjust. A Wolfen was, after all, the ultimate human adaptation.

Julianna would prepare some trick, or some test of his loyalty. Of that, he was sure. The biggest advantage Wolfen had was human ignorance, but Julianna knew... too much. She'd be a small challenge for his skills.

Sunday's showdown would mark his inauguration day, the anointing of the new Alpha!

# Chapter Thirty-One

"I had a good time this evening, Sis. That was a good idea you had," Julianna said on the ride home.

"I had fun too, but I didn't like the lying, or at least omitting part of the plan, and I think the guys suspect something."

"How could they? I don't like leaving them out either, but we've buried both our mother and my best friend in the past few weeks, and your life, no, both of our lives, are in jeopardy. We're not doing anything to hurt them. I couldn't do that. If there's one man in the world I could picture myself with in twenty years, it is Chase Graves, damn it!" And there lay the conundrum. It was only a few short months ago that she considered Chase the last man on earth she'd share her life or bed with – for even one night. Now she wanted to be with him forever, but there was that nagging doubt about him that made her put up her guard.

"Jase is so trusting, so …" Lorelei began.

"I know how you feel. I've seen how Jase looks at you, too, but we have to protect ourselves, just in case."

"I know, I know. It just doesn't feel right."

"Yeah, it feels deceitful, devious and disloyal –all the relationship-destroying Ds. That's not how you should treat friends." Julianna shrugged.

"Yes, my exact thoughts too."

"But if we get through this, we never have to feel that way with them again."

Back at the cabin, they discussed the nuances of their plan, trying to pick up on any holes or hidden dangers. They sipped wine as they went through the strategy, step by step.

"I'm beat." Julianna yawned and drained the last sip from her glass.

"Yeah, I think it's time we called it a night," Lorelei agreed.

Sleep did not come easy for Julianna, who sat on the edge of her bed in her room, elbows on her knees, chin resting on her hands.

*Oh Chase, why am I falling for you? Your timing really sucks.* Lorelei was right. How would they get past this duplicity so early in their relationship? She closed her eyes and felt Chase's strong arms holding her, comforting her through all of her trials. How could she doubt him? *You know why, and it's time to let it go, if you can.*

"I really am scared of him, of us," she admitted to the walls, and to herself. "It's not just what he might be, but what he awakens in me, and how he makes me feel."

She dropped her head to the pillow. What was she going to do? Why should Chase trust her, when she hadn't earned, and certainly didn't deserve, his trust? She asked him to risk his life, and fed him enough lies to choke on.

This wasn't who she was, not who she wanted to be. She wouldn't allow fear to rule her! Tomorrow she would call Shane, make sure all was going as planned for Sunday. Then, and if Lorelei agreed, she'd call Chase, sweet, caring Chase, and come clean. The decision brought her peace, and she slept.

*It was time to trust again.*

# Chapter Thirty-Two

The next morning, Julianna looked up from the table as Lorelei walked into the kitchen and went to the coffee pot. After pouring herself a cup, she sat across from her sister.

"I think we should tell them everything." Julianna said abruptly.

"The guys? So you suddenly think it's safe to tell them? They'll be pissed that we left that part out."

"Better sooner than later, don't you think? I don't want to go into this with them in the dark, and it wasn't a big deal, just a minor tweak to the plan."

"Okay, let's tell them. I wish you told me last night so I could've slept, but show me the freaking root cellar first."

"After my coffee."

The cellar was every bit as bad as Julianna's description. They slipped on elbow-length gloves, and pulled away the poison ivy and honeysuckle vines. Both of them heaved at the heavy steel door, and the rusted hinges groaned in protest.

"I guess I don't have a lot of incentive to get in that place." Lorelei pushed the hair away from her eyes.

Another pull, and Julianna looked down at the yellowed concrete walls, heavily marked with the progression of moss and mold. Two inches of foul-smelling stagnant water covered the floor, and she heard the steady *plop- plop* as more dripped in.

"Really?" Lorelei asked. "What if it rains? Does it flood? My toes will look like a Granny's after a night in there!"

Julianna couldn't look at her sister. She wasn't sure if she could handle a whole night imprisoned in that hole either.

"Well, it's just for the one night, and Jase will be here to keep me company. Show me how the latches work."

Julianna showed her the order of release for the bolts and throws to escape after she and Jase transitioned back, in case she and Chase didn't make it in time.

"Okay, I'm calling Shane now," Julianna said. "After that, the fun part – not!"

They went back inside, Julianna retrieved her cellphone from her bedroom, and stepped out to the porch. She had three missed calls from Chase already. He must have enjoyed last night too, she thought with a smile, and dialed Shane's number.

"Hey, Julianna! I was just thinking about you."

"Only good things, I hope."

"Of course! What else could they be? I'm looking forward to Sunday. It's been too long."

"For me too. It's hard to find a guy you can trust."

Shane laughed.

"What's so funny? Are you suggesting your intentions are less than honorable?"

"No, not at all, and it's nothing, really. I just remembered your Dad saying the same thing years ago."

"You knew my father?"

"A little. He was good friends with my dad. They went hunting and fishing together, and sometimes I tagged along. One time I overheard him telling my dad that his friends had turned against him, and he didn't know who to trust any more. He and dad were pretty tight."

"I didn't know."

"Yeah, but now that I think about it, you repeating your father's words isn't so funny, not those words anyway. It was a long time ago, but if I remember right, your father was killed shortly after that conversation.

Please be careful, Julianna, you mean a lot to me. You know you can call me anytime, for anything."

Julianna heard the beep and glanced at her phone. Chase's number popped up.

"I know. Thank you Shane, and I do appreciate you. You're always there for me, but I'm fine. I really just called to say hello, and to make sure we were still on for Sunday afternoon."

"You bet we are. All the beasts of the forest couldn't keep me from your door, my lady." He laughed.

"All the beasts of…"

"Yeah, you know, like the medieval days, what the knights might tell some worthy damsel about the ogres and dragons? A bad joke. Sorry."

"Oh, okay. I'm really looking forward to it. It gets pretty lonely out here, just Lorelei and me."

"Will Lorelei be there too? That would be great. I mean… if she joins us for dinner."

"Now that wouldn't be very romantic." Julianna chuckled. "No, Lorelei will be here, but she said she'll be gracious enough to sequester herself in her room that night, in case we…well, just in case."

"That sounds good to me. Let me know if anything changes, but I'll plan to be at your door, three o'clock sharp, wine bottle in hand."

"Sounds like a plan. See you then, Shane." Julianna hung up, and took a deep breath to prepare for her call to Chase.

"Lorelei, can you come out here? I could use the moral support." Julianna pressed the dial button.

# Chapter Thirty-Three

Chase swung the axe and split the large chunk of oak with the first blow. He told Jase he was getting an early start on next year's firewood, but in truth, he needed to blow off some steam after what his brother told him last night.

He knew Julianna didn't trust them, or him at least, but he never thought she'd turn on him. It cast a whole new light on their relationship, on Sunday's plan, and on everything. How do you protect someone who wants you dead? Or wants to throw your brother into some dark, damp hole?

Again and again he swung the axe, added another piece of wood to the chopping block, and swung again. He'd split half of a cord since breakfast, which he choked down in a hurry to get outside to avoid talking about it with Jase.

He heard the screen door open and knew he couldn't avoid Jase any longer. He rested the head of the axe on his booted foot, caught his breath, and looked up at the house as Jase's head appeared.

"Hey, Chase? Your phone has been steady buzzing for an hour. I think you might want to take this. It's Julianna."

Chase threw the axe down on the pile of wood that still needed to be split. "What the hell. I'm not sure I can pretend everything's just fine and dandy. No, that's bullshit, I won't pretend."

He went into the house, grabbed the phone, and the buzzing began again. He waited for Julianna's number to appear, and he pressed the accept button.

"Yeah?" he answered.

"Chase? I just got off the phone with Shane. Everything is going exactly as we planned."

"Like *you* planned, you mean?"

"Well, yeah, but it's a good plan, don't you think?"

"The parts I know are."

"What? Look, Chase, I need to talk to you about something, and I don't want to do it over the phone. Can you meet me somewhere?"

Chase paused. Was this another one of her tricks? Maybe she and Shane planned to ambush him before Sunday. That would explain the image Jase saw in Lorelei's mind. Julianna pointing a gun at his chest while Shane looked on.

"Chase? Did I lose you? Can you hear me?"

"I'm here. I'll meet you at the shed. I guess you remember the one I mean."

"It's broad daylight. Anyone could see us go in."

"And nobody can see us once we're inside."

"Chase, are you okay? You don't sound right."

"I'll meet you there in a half hour." He disconnected.

# Chapter Thirty-Four

"Oh, damn it all to hell," Julianna groaned.

"What, Jules? He knows? How?"

"He knows *something*. You and Jase with that image-sensing, mind-reading, whatever Wolfen bullshit. Were you thinking about it when we went back to the table?"

"Of course I was. I'm not used to other people being able to do that. I didn't think, I ..."

"I don't know what he saw, and it's not your fault, Lor, but you should have heard him on the phone. He was as cold as a freezer full of icicles."

"Then you better warm him back up. I don't think you can do it without his help. Tell him how you really feel."

"I know. I'm going to meet him now, to explain and apologize."

"Good luck!"

Julianna drove too fast for the mountain roads, but she'd known every bend since she was a teenager. She learned about all the new potholes since she'd returned, and she used that knowledge to advantage. She slid her car to a stop in front of Jose's shed, right beside Chase's truck, walked to the door, and stepped inside.

Chase stood sharpening a carving gouge, his face bristly with whiskers. "Come on in, Julianna. Just touching up a few of Jose's tools. He's kind of particular about them."

"Look, Chase, I'm sorry. I don't know what you know, or think you know, but I wanted to talk to you today anyway. Lorelei and I both felt guilty about leaving a part of the plan out. I was going to tell you everything."

"So tell me." He didn't take his eyes away from the strop.

"I told you the real plan, except about the part where Jase and Lorelei will be. I'm sorry I didn't trust you enough, and I feel terrible about it. Well, I did trust you, but I had to be sure. Lorelei and Jase will be locked in our root cellar. It's strong, and it's scent-proof. Shane won't know they're in there."

"And I wouldn't know either? That was the plan? That's the black hole you were going to throw my brother into?"

"Yes, that's all. I wouldn't do anything to hurt you, Chase. You know that!"

"I know my brother saw an image of you pointing a pistol at my chest while Shane watched. What part of the plan was that?"

"It's not. Well only if you transformed instead of Shane. It was a backup plan if everything turned to shit. If you were the one." Julianna dropped her eyes to the floor.

Chase set down the gouge and faced her. "Do you always have a back-up plan, Julianna? Something to rely on instead of trust?" His face softened, and his eyes implored her. "You are my very soul, but how can I trust you now? I have to think about Jase too, about leaving him defenseless."

Julianna smiled, though a tear streaked down her cheek and slowly began releasing the buttons on her blouse. "Maybe I can prove it?" She dropped the shirt to the floor.

"As much as I'd like to, that doesn't prove anything."

"What then? What can I do? I swear if you will just believe me… I need you, Chase."

Chase didn't answer, but his eyes never wandered from her breasts. "I don't know, Jules. I want to believe in you, I really do. I want nothing more, and I want nothing or no one more than I do you." He walked over and embraced her.

Julianna's eyes watered, but she stepped away. Her hands tugged at her belt, and Chase shook his head.

She stared into his eyes. "Lorelei told me to be honest with you, and tell you how I feel. My baby sister isn't such a baby any more. So here goes. I think I love you, Chase Graves. I can't be more honest and vulnerable than that. You're probably thinking that I would say or do anything to keep you on our side, but not this."

She stepped over to the wood sling, and placed her wrists inside, as tears streamed down her face.

"Pull the rope, Chase," she said with a sob, but she held her head up high. "You should know I'm terrified of being helpless, at anyone's mercy. It's my greatest fear, but I'll do it if it will prove we can trust each other."

Chase loosened the sling and pulled it from her wrists. "No, I won't do anything you don't want, or anything to cause you pain. There is something, though, one thing that will prove your trust, and inspire mine."

Julianna looked at him, and waited.

"Tell me the deep, dark secret that you pretend doesn't exist. Tell me what happened, who hurt you, why you've trusted no one for so many years. Then we can start fresh."

# Chapter Thirty-Five

"Chase, I'd have to relive my whole senior year, and we don't have time now. I'll tell you later, I promise."

"I've got plenty of time. Let's get comfortable on the couch." He took her hand and led her to the scene of their recent lovemaking.

"Chase, I can't…"

"Please, Jules." He gently pushed her down onto the couch, and he sat next to her.

She considered denying it, or making up a story, but his caring look of shared suffering filled her heart and wouldn't allow anything but truth.

"Chase, you were a high school jock, a star quarterback. I can't expect you to understand what it was like being a Native American teenager in an all-white high school."

"Try me."

Julianna shrugged her shoulders and sighed. "Okay, add in the mysterious death of my father, and my mother, who the kids all called crazy and were probably right. Well, I wasn't very popular, except as the brunt of jokes.

"I was a flat-chested bookworm, a late-blooming non-entity, except for the acknowledgement of being Lorelei's older sister. She always was the social butterfly. My only girlfriend was Carla Sanchez, another class pariah, and we were best friends. We bandaged each other's spiritual wounds through most of the four-year torture they call high school.

"In October of my senior year, Mom decided to throw a sixteenth birthday party for me. I didn't care that she didn't realize it was actually my seventeenth birthday, just having one was enough for me. She invited the whole class, and a couple from Lorelei's too. We didn't have a lot of money, but we spent the week before crafting decorations, and Mom made a cake big enough to feed an army.

"All of Lorelei's friends came, but from my senior class only Ben Fisher, Carla, and Missy Rhodes showed up. Six months later, we were still eating frozen leftover birthday cake. I was glad Carla came. She'd been distant since the summer when she started hanging out with Missy's crowd, and I felt a little left out. Missy coming was the real surprise though. She was an elitist little rich bitch, and the most popular girl in our class, homecoming queen, prom queen and all that crap."

"So, what about this Ben guy? You haven't mentioned him before. An old boyfriend?"

"Yeah, I guess he was. Ben was kind of a nerd, so not really my type, but I didn't know what my type was back then. Any boy who would give me the time of day I guess, and he was the first one to show any interest in me. Carla said Missy twisted his arm to come to my party, told him we'd be good together, and I thought we were. We had a lot of interests in common, and he showed me a lot of attention. He kissed me under the big oak in the backyard that day. My first kiss." Julianna gave him a sheepish look.

"Your first kiss was when you were a senior?"

Julianna felt her face flush. "I believed *you*, Chase."

"No, I didn't mean it that way. I'm sorry, but you are the most beautiful woman I've ever known, and it's hard for me to wrap my head around it."

Julianna searched his face and saw no deception there. "So you thought I was always a beautiful seductress, who could twist any man to her every desire?" She rolled her eyes.

"This man anyway. I don't care about any others, except that they hurt you… their loss. Tell me the rest."

"I used to take my chest measurements every weekend, hoping to see the mark on the tape measure stretch, and late in senior year it happened. My boobs started filling out, my hormones finally kicked in, or maybe Ben squeezing and pawing at my chest for five months swelled them up. But all the boys noticed."

"So was Ben your first…"

"No. We talked on the phone for hours every night. When we ran out of things to say, we just breathed at each other. I really thought he was the guy for me, Chase, that it might be forever, but copping a feel, well, a lot of feels, was a far as it ever went. I was a good girl, or maybe I was just a chicken shit.

"I started getting a lot of male attention I wasn't used to, and I enjoyed it. Maybe I got a bit full of myself. Carla wanted to do stuff with me again, and guys who hadn't spoken to me in four years hung around my locker. Lee Bailey was one of them. He was a first-string forward on our varsity basketball team, and Missy's boyfriend.

"One day I was carrying my books and a science project, and I dropped the damn report in the hallway. A mob of kids were hustling to class, stepping all over my stuff. I was on my hands and knees trying to snatch it up before it got ruined. Then an extra set of hands appeared, helping, and I looked up. It was Lee, and he offered to help me carry everything to class. I didn't see anything wrong with that. I needed the help, but Missy didn't see it that way. She confronted me in the locker room and said I didn't have what it took to steal her boyfriend. That I wasn't woman enough to hold the nerd I had, and she slapped me. In front of the whole locker room, she slapped me! I didn't even think. I grabbed her, tossed her over a bench, and jumped on top of her. Years of snide remarks and put-downs welled up in me, and I wanted to beat her senseless, but luckily they pulled us apart before I did any real damage. That marked the end of my short-lived popularity.

"Missy started all kinds of rumors about me after that. She said I was a whore, an Indian squaw slut, to be precise. A few of her male thralls lied and said they'd slept with me, that I had all manner of diseases, and that I wasn't any good at sex, of course."

"What a bitch. I knew a few girls like that. I wish you'd knocked her teeth down her throat." Chase held her hands in his. "I'm sorry, Jules, I didn't know. They ruined senior year for you?"

"A year of eating alone, everyone stopping to stare at me in the hallways and whispering behind my back, my reputation in ruins, of course. Oh, but that was just their warm-up. There's more if you really want to hear it. You need to if you really want to understand."

Chase nodded.

With red eyes leaking tears, Julianna continued. "My first semester break in my freshman year of college, I came home feeling like my whole life stretched out before me. I went to lunch in town one day, and I met up with my old buddy Carla. She told me how much she missed me and the old times we had together; how bad she felt over ignoring me after my tribulations started. She said she hated the way Missy destroyed my senior year, and she still wanted to get even with her. I told her I didn't care about Missy. High school was well behind us, and my fresh beginning in college had already begun.

"Carla asked if Ben and I would come to a dance that some teen group in the county put on. I felt like I was a little too mature for teen dances being a college girl, at the ripe old age of eighteen, but she assured me lots of our old classmates and some other couples our age would be there. Anyway, she pretty much guilt-tripped me into going.

"Ben and I weren't really together anymore. We emailed each other and had an occasional phone call, but I called him up and we ended up going to the dance together. We danced a few times, and then he excused himself to go to the bathroom. Carla moved over to sit beside me, and I noticed Ben slip out of the side door of the auditorium. I figured he was sneaking a smoke.

"Two more songs played, and Carla tugged at my arm. 'I want to show you something,' she said. 'It's time Little Miss Missy got hers.'

"I told her I wasn't interested, but I was still foolish enough to follow her outside, through the parking lot to the thick hedges. It was a well-known spot for drinking and making out during these dances, and from what I could hear, someone was putting it to use. I stopped, but Carla tugged at my arm.

"'You've got to see this,' she said, and like a chump, I followed along. There was a bare place in the middle of the hedges about half the size of our kitchen in the cabin. When we were almost on top of the moans and groans, Carla stopped and pushed me in. I tripped and fell forward, face first, inches away from Ben. His was on his back doing the dirty with my old friend Missy. He didn't even open his eyes to notice me. Missy looked at me and slapped him.

"'Leave him alone, Missy. He never did anything to you,' I said.

"Missy slapped him again. 'Ben, do you want me to stop?'

"'Fine, enjoy each other.' I turned to get out of there, but Carla and Felicity Barnes blocked my exit. I pushed past them, but they caught my arms and twisted them behind my back. I felt a pop in my shoulder, and the two of them dragged me back into the clearing, kicking and yelling.

"Missy finished with Ben, walked over, and slapped me in the face. Ben never moved. He had his arm across his eyes in some post-sexual stupor.

"'Who did you think you were fucking with, Pocahontas?' she said. 'You knew Lee was spoken for.'

"I said something like, 'Are you still harping on that? Let me be, Missy. We can call it even. We've long since graduated, and we don't have to even see each other again.'

"By then a small crowd had gathered. Missy wouldn't let it go and asked the other girls to back her up. Felicity accused me of stuffing my bra and putting on airs.

"Two other girls who I didn't know joined in on the fun and helped them strip off my skirt and blouse. They tied my hands to a tree behind my back. I fought them, Chase, and I yelled, but no one came, not then. I managed to kick one of the new girls in the forehead, and Carla caught my elbow to her eye, but I was too weak to hold them all off. They were strong and determined. Why were they doing this? I never did anything to them.

"When I was exhausted, I just stood there crying like a baby, and everyone left me there like that."

"Oh, sweet Jesus. Jules!" Chase's skin turned pale.

Julianna dropped her eyes to the sawdust-covered floor. "I was terrified, naked and helpless, and betrayed. I was at their mercy, and weak, like when my father died, and when Mom went insane. They weren't just staring at my nakedness, but into me. The vulnerable secrets of my soul, my innermost fears and weaknesses, were laid bare for their amusement. Their eyes glassed over, and their faces were masks of depraved joy. As horrible as it was, they'd been in no hurry to end my torment. They stole my humanity. I knew they'd come back for more taunting and to revel in my humiliation.

"That's when the parade of my ex-classmates began. Never more than two at a time, so they wouldn't attract the chaperones' attention. They came to see the foolish girl who stood up to Missy, stripped bare for their enjoyment. Flashlights in hand so they wouldn't miss any detail, pointing and laughing at me!

"And the two people I trusted most in the world? My boyfriend Ben never made any move to help me. Ben, who'd once sworn his eternal love and devotion to me, sat in the shadows watching. He looked like he was having fun, waiting to see what they'd do to me next.

"My best friend Carla? The girl I'd shared my most secret and sacred thoughts and desires with? She and Missy giggled and had a grand old time.

"I was wishing I could just die right there when I heard Lee's voice. 'What the fuck are you doing to her, Missy? I told you nothing happened. Julianna is just a nice girl.' He grabbed her arm and ordered her and the others – sick perverts, he called them – to get the hell out of there. Except for Carla, for whom he had even more disgust, because she supposedly was my friend. He told her to help me – or else!

"That's when the band announced their last song, an oldie but a goody, and the last of the spectators from my little show fled inside, including Missy and Ben. Carla stayed behind, untied me, and as the band started cranking out 'Love Hurts,' I pulled my clothes back on as fast as I could.

"Carla said, 'This was very hard for me tonight too, Julianna, but an important lesson for you, I think. Never mess with another woman's man. No real harm was done, and hey, you do have a pretty hot body. No hard feelings?' She held out her hand to help me up. I took it, then kneed her in the belly and spit in her face. I walked the five miles home, holding my clothes together, and getting off the road whenever a car passed.

"When I got home, my mother was sitting at the kitchen table waiting for me. She saw me, saw my clothes, and I ran to her in tears hoping for comfort. She slapped me and called me a whore. I packed some things and left, pitching a tent by the river that night. It was a long time before I ever went back to the cabin.

"Something changed in me that night, Chase. I'd never again be the sweet innocent weak little girl I'd been. I swore I'd get stronger, strong enough to right wrongs, and never be a victim again, never trust again.

"I caught Missy alone a few weeks later by the river, and I hurt her, but not as much as I'd planned. Somewhere between bloodying her pert little nose and splitting her too-perfect lips, I realized she wasn't the one who hurt me. I didn't even like Missy, and didn't expect much better from her, but Ben and Carla? They were the only friends I'd ever had."

# Chapter Thirty-Six

"I'll get even with them, Jules, so help me God." Chase slammed his fist on the coffee table.

"No you won't. It's all in the past. Besides, karma or whatever caught up with them. Ben went into computers, and got caught stealing his company's secrets. They pressed charges, and he's currently locked up. He'll be lucky to find work slinging burgers when he gets out.

"Carla didn't have the scores to get into college. She tried community college part-time and flunked out. She had a kid and started turning tricks to meet expenses, but she caught AIDS, Chase. I wouldn't wish that on anyone."

"And the Missy bitch?"

"Missy's gone, but nobody knows where. Lee dumped her after that night, and she left town before the summer was over. Even her mother doesn't know what happened to her, or where she went. She could be dead now for all I know."

Chase nodded his head, but wished for any revenge he might extract, knowing it was his conscience causing his reaction. He was really angry at himself. Where was he when she needed him? He should have fulfilled his promise to Thane. What could possibly have been more important than protecting this beautiful, precious woman sitting before him, spilling her heart, and sharing her horrid experience? Nothing. He looked at her reddened eyes, washed repeatedly by the tears of her pent up agony from long ago. Nothing was more important than keeping that hurt from flooding her eyes and heart.

He didn't know where he was, or what he was doing the night of that dance. He knew as long as his heart beat in his chest, he'd never let anyone cause her such suffering again. For now, that would have to be enough.

"I'm so sorry, Jules. That's a terrible secret to hold inside, but I understand why you did. I know you trust me, and my trust in you is renewed, but I…I should have been there!" He turned his face away from her and choked back a sob. Her tortured ordeal was his fault. He could have, should have, been there.

"You're here now. And I need you just as much now as then." She sat on his lap, and for a few moments, they held each other, sharing the wounds of that night.

"I've never told anyone else what happened, Chase. But I'm glad I told you. I've been afraid I would be the one judged and found wanting. Your understanding means more to me than you know."

He kissed her neck, and she nuzzled his ear. Chase felt his immediate response at her mere touch. Only Julianna, he thought.

"Love me, Chase? Show me?"

"Oh sweet Jesus, I do. I want to show you every moment for the rest of my life."

His lips found hers, and each tasted the other's tongue. Clothes fell away and they both felt the heat in the other's skin.

As they moved as one, it was as if they'd been together forever. That both always knew exactly what the other needed. More than a physical attraction, more than a mere release, they felt their souls touch and rise to heights neither had ever known before.

Drained of thought, and their reserves ripped away, the lovers clung to each other. Their bodies seemed to meld together, to become one being, with the same thoughts, the same needs.

Chase held her close in the aftermath, reveling in their bond, their surrender to each other. *My God, what a woman.* True, his experience was limited in one way, but still he knew. There was only one woman for him, and that was Jules.

He wondered if Thane knew this, and if somehow he always knew. And did the knowledge make him happy?

# Chapter Thirty-Seven

Shane hurried to his car. He didn't want to be late tonight, not on this full moon of destiny. At long last, Julianna would see him for what he was, no more doubt or deceit.

When her cabin loomed ahead, he coasted to a stop and grabbed the bottle of wine from under the seat. He opened his door carefully, quietly. His mother always said an ounce of prevention was worth a pound of cure, and even though she didn't follow her own advice, he didn't plan to be ambushed.

Shane crept forward, testing his footing before committing his weight. Besides the dangers of human interference, there was the myriad of Thane's rejuvenated booby traps to contend with. He circled the cabin, observing, and testing the air. He sniffed out the hint of freshly turned dirt near the old root cellar. The sister's scent trails moved to and from the cellar, but no other smell lingered there. He easily side-stepped a snare, and again caught Lorelei's scent, leading away from the cabin. She'd be back soon if not already, he thought. She wouldn't be outside tonight after sunset. And moonrise!

When satisfied it was safe to enter, he stepped lightly onto the porch. He peered through the window and saw Julianna at the kitchen table chopping vegetables.

"Julianna?" he called and knocked on the door.

He heard her stocking feet running across the floor boards. She threw open the door, and greeted him with a hug.

"Shane! And you remembered the wine!"

"It was your only request, and a small gift, although I did have to arm wrestle my father to get another bottle of his private reserve."

Julianna laughed, and Shane followed her to the kitchen.

"How do you like your steak, Shane? I have a pair of thick T-bones ready for the grill. Would you like to do the honors? I tend to burn them, and I hate burnt steak."

"Me too. Rare to medium rare – anything else destroys the flavor. The taste is in the blood, you know."

While Julianna nuked the veggies, Shane fired up the grill. When the meat and vegetables were done, Julianna had the table set, bread sliced, and wine poured for them both.

"This is fantastic, Julianna. I didn't realize how hungry I was until just now." He took a sip of wine and noticed Julianna watching him. He didn't miss the slight upturn of the corner of her mouth as she took a sip from her own glass.

"So, shouldn't we have Lorelei join us? I feel bad making her hide out in her own home."

"No, she went out with some friends. Knowing Lorelei, it will be late when she gets home, but that will give us some time to ourselves."

Shane regarded her with one eyebrow raised. "I guess we should eat up then."

They made small talk about the weather and their classes at school while they ate. After dinner, Julianna suggested they would be more comfortable in the living room.

"Okay, but let me help clean up first."

"No, I've got it. You're my guest."

"Oh, wow," Shane said when he stood up, and grabbed the table for balance. "Hmm, don't know where that came from. I'm a bit dizzy."

"Can you make it to the living room? I'll help you."

When Shane was settled on the couch, Julianna retrieved their wine.

"I'm not sure I can handle any more wine just yet, Julianna. Would you mind getting me a glass of water?"

"Of course. I'll be right back."

As she turned into the hallway, Shane pulled out a small envelope from his pants pocket and dumped the contents in Julianna's wine. Stupid bitch, did she think he wouldn't notice the wine in her glass was a different color than the wine he brought? At least she'd figured out that his father's "special reserve" wine contained some extra potency. He'd give her credit for that, but she couldn't know Wolfen were immune to the home-grown drug in the wine. He smiled with satisfaction.

The dried vaginal fluids of an estrus werewolf made humans lose their inhibitions, corrupted their sense of balance and time, and it hindered their problem-solving ability. How could she know that it just makes werewolves horny?

He heard Julianna approach and leaned back on the couch with his hands covering his face. Julianna handed him the glass of water, and he took a big swallow

"I hope it wasn't my cooking. Has this ever happened to you before?"

"No, but the water is helping. If my head doesn't clear up, I'll hit the road and get back home for some sleep, but I think I'll be fine. Actually, I feel damn good, except for being dizzy."

Julianna leaned into him, kissed his lower lip, and sucked it in gently. "I'm glad." She dropped her hand to his crotch.

Shane jumped up, and slapped her hard in the face, knocking her to the floor. Xena flew into the room from her spot in the doorway and barked at Shane's feet. He drew back his leg and kicked the little dog across the room.

"What the hell was that for?" Julianna wiped at the blood seeping from her lips, as she ran over to her dog.

"So you thought it was me you shot in the balls? It was my brother, Garret, you shot, not me. And thanks for that, by the way. That silver bullet wound will never heal."

"I wish a bullet had found you as well!" Julianna bent over to inspect Xena.

"Julianna, Julianna… how stupid do you think I am? I saw through your plan. Drug me? Seduce me into letting my guard down, then what? Oh yeah, I guess your lame-ass protector comes charging in? Yeah, that figures, he's afraid to face me unless I'm stoned. Sorry to disappoint you, but I like my plan better."

Julianna determined Xena had no serious injury and tried to stand to confront Shane, but her legs wouldn't cooperate. She plopped down to the floor on her butt.

"I imagine you're starting to feel the effects now. Just relax, and everything will be fine. It's what you've really wanted anyway. Everything you've done since high school led you here, to being my slut, and your sister, my queen. Speaking of high school, I have a special surprise for you. Missy, get in here!"

The front door opened, and Missy Rhodes walked in smiling.

"Hey, girlfriend. Long time, no see."

Julianna's mouth fell open as she stared at the woman.

"Oh yeah, it's your old buddy, all right." Shane laughed.

"Did you miss me?" Missy stepped over to Julianna and sat on her legs, straddling her. She grabbed the front of Julianna's blouse and twisted her left breast. "Tell the truth, that's what you really missed, isn't it? You liked the rough stuff, huh, slut?"

"Enough, Missy, we have a lot to do before moonrise. Don't worry, Julianna. We'll take good care of you, and we'll see to it that Lorelei is taken care of too. I doubt she's very far away."

Julianna pushed Missy off her and used a heavy floor lamp to pull herself to her feet. She reached under her blouse for the knife concealed in her belt and pointed it at her tormentors, holding onto the lamp with her other hand for support. "Stay away from me!"

"You wish!" Missy grabbed a book from the coffee table and held it in both hands as she rushed at her. At the last moment, Julianna let go of the lamp and sidestepped her, sticking the blade in her side before falling to the floor.

Missy screamed. "You fucking whore bitch. I'll kill you!" She pulled the blade out.

Shane snatched Missy's wrist before she could strike, prying the weapon from her hand. He slapped her and she fell back on the couch. "Now ladies, let's play nice, at least for a little while longer." He smiled at Julianna as her eyesight dimmed and quickly went black.

# Chapter Thirty-Eight

Chase reached the cabin earlier than they'd planned. It was hard enough to absent himself during Shane's arrival, but necessary. If Shane sensed him there, all bets were off, and their plan would fail. Shane had to accept Julianna's innocence, or at least her indecision about him. His wolf senses would not allow him to walk into an ambush.

The house lights were off, which gave him pause. The sun wouldn't set for a couple of hours yet, but the cabin was on the east side of the mountain. *Julianna might want to be alone with him in the dark. Shut up, Chase. Don't be stupid.*

Besides the absence of lights, and his own jealousy, something else had his stomach in knots. Something wasn't right. But what? Then it came to him – the quiet. That was what was wrong! The always starving blue jays weren't at Julianna's bird feeders, and the pesky squirrels, likewise, were conspicuous by their absence.

He didn't pause to wonder what Thane would do, and he didn't consider their well laid-out plan. With his .45 in hand, he ran to the porch, turned the doorknob slowly, then violently pushed the door open. He rushed into the dark living room, gun at the ready. Silence.

He ran from room to room. Not with the proper tactical approach, but in a foolish, full-bore, uncompromising, kill-or-be-killed assault mode. He heard a noise from the living room and dashed in with his pistol leading the way.

Xena was curled up in a ball on the floor whining. "What the hell did he do to you, little girl?"

Xena licked at his hands as he felt her over for any broken bones.

"You're gonna be okay, girl." He carried her to Julianna's room and closed the door behind him as he left.

"Julianna! Where are you?"

He ran outside to the root cellar and listened at the door. He didn't hear Jase or Lorelei, but the door appeared undisturbed. He reached for the handle, but reconsidered. They had their own demons to fight tonight. They didn't need another worry, and wouldn't be any help in their coming condition anyway.

Chase went back to the cabin, turned on the lights, and began again, searching for clues. The dirty plates and glasses in the kitchen sink proved they got as far as finishing dinner. That was when Julianna was going to make her move and drug Shane. He found the half-empty bottle of wine on the counter, along with two empty wine glasses. So far, so good.

In the living room carpet were two long indentations leading to the front door. Drag marks from someone's heels? He detected the aroma of a perfume he'd not smelled before, not on Julianna or Lorelei.

He turned his attention to the couch and saw the bloody knife, Julianna's knife, embedded in one of Helena's decorative pillows. It held a small note:

"Thane picked a pair of real losers. The women are ours. S."

# Chapter Thirty-Nine

"Shhh, there's someone out there," Jase said.

"I didn't hear anything," Lorelei whispered.

"No, or smell anything either, but someone's still out there. I can feel them."

"Is it Julianna? Or Chase?"

"I can't tell, but they're moving away now. One or both of them checking up on us maybe."

"We have a little time yet. Maybe we should do something to make it worth their concern." Lorelei giggled and licked her lips.

"Lor, do you take anything seriously?"

"Oh no, you did not just ask me that, Jase Graves. Not you of all people. You'd laugh, drink beer, and roast hotdogs while your house burned down!"

"Maybe, well not quite that extreme, but I'll own it. Maybe we're too much alike. This place really brings me down. I feel lost and hopeless down here. Don't you feel it?"

"Yeah, but I'm just a poor low-life Initiate. I'd bet it's worse for you."

"And here I am complaining, with a drop-dead gorgeous, scantily clad woman, alone in a dark hole where anything could happen. But all the while my brother and your sister are risking their lives for us. I hate that part of it, Lor."

"What other option do we have?"

"I don't know. Chase was always the go-to guy. The guy you wanted on your team during the game and on your side when things got rough. Me, I'm the class clown kind of guy. Guess I'll never grow up, just like my father always said."

"How badly do you want it? To be able to help I mean?"

"More than anything at the moment. Even after they take Shane out, they are way outnumbered. Two against how many?"

"I have something that might help." Lorelei handed Jase a small vial.

# Chapter Forty

"She'll wake soon, Missy. I'm going back for the Initiate. I have the altar rock ready for her, and Julianna will have a front row seat. Remember, we want them unmarked until the pack arrives, and the change comes. Then we will take them both." Shane grinned.

"I'll watch the little whore, Shane, my Alpha to be. What a team we will make!"

Shane checked the ropes binding Julianna's arms to the tree, and satisfied they'd hold – even against a wolf – he walked back toward the cabin. Did the spoiled little rich bitch Missy really think he'd consider someone as weak as she was to rule beside him? Missy going from his father's slave to Alpha female of the pack would certainly shake things up, but to pass her anemic genes on to the next generation of Wolfen? No, when he became Alpha, Missy would become a martyr to the new order.

He quickly retraced his steps, pausing in the area of the root cellar. He smelled no trace of the Initiate inside, but the scent trail around the doorway was unmistakable. He reached down and snatched the handle, but the door didn't budge.

"I have your sister, Lorelei. I'll kill her if you don't open the door now. You know I will. I know where Thane kept his power tools, and if I remember correctly, there's even a stick or two of TNT in his closet."

There was no answer from inside. Shane yanked again at the door handle, and again, it remained unmoved. He grunted as he kicked it.

"Fuck you, Lorelei. I *will* get in!" He stomped away and made for the cabin. He was indeed aware of where Thane stored his tools and the dynamite, but he needed neither. He stepped into the first bedroom he came to and grabbed a clothes hanger from the closet. Thane had used the same lock his father installed on his own cage to appease his weak mother. It could be opened from the outside with the key or from inside with the latch. Malcolm taught him to pick it when he was no more than a child.

The lock took longer than he remembered, probably from years of disuse, he thought. Only two simple latches, it shouldn't be so hard! But then came the satisfying click as the last latch slipped free.

Shane grabbed the handle for a third time, and snatched it up and away. The door crashed back against its hinges, and he looked inside.

Lorelei stood chained by the wall, a desperate look of fear in her eyes.

"You have nothing to fear, little one. In fact, you'll be the star of our show tonight. You are to be revered as my new queen."

He jumped down in the hole beside her.

"Where's the key, Lorelei?"

"Shane, don't do this. I'll do anything you want, but don't do this!"

"Key, Lorelei? No? Very well, I'll find it myself." Shane ripped the front of her blouse open. "Very nice!" He lifted the leather thong that led down into her bra, and pulled out the key. "Now, that wasn't so hard, was it?"

"Please, Shane, don't…"

"I'm surprised you're alone here, Lorelei. I really expected to find your traitor-ass boyfriend here too. Sort of a two-fer, but it's no matter, come along."

As he hoisted her up and out of the hole, she broke free and ran for the woods, but he tackled her before she'd made it halfway.

"Easy or hard, Lorelei. Your call."

"I know what kind of man your father is, and I know how hard it must have been for you growing up, but you don't have to do this. I can still be your queen."

"It's the hard way then." Shane drew back his hand to hit her.

"No! I'll be good, what do you want?"

He picked her up, slung her across his shoulders, and entered the woods.

# Chapter Forty-One

Jules awakened slowly. There were sounds of people moving around her, but her eyes were foggy. She tried to wipe them clear, but her hands wouldn't move far enough. They were bound. She tried her legs, and they moved freely. Where was she? What happened? She remembered having dinner with Shane…Missy…Missy Rhodes was there! *Shane drugged me!*

She kept her eyes open, but only a slit. It wouldn't do to let them know she was regaining consciousness. She recognized Shane's voice, and yes, Missy's too, and somehow that was even worse. Where was Chase? Did Shane get him too? At least she knew Jase and Lorelei were safe.

"Shane, do you have to tie me up? I'll be good. I promise!" Lorelei's voice! Julianna heard cloth ripping and Lorelei's whimper.

"Please, please don't! You don't have to do this!" Lorelei said. *What were they doing to her?*

"I'm sorry, Lorelei, but I do have to. In fact, I want to."

Julianna turned her head and saw the blurred image of her sister. They were tying her spread eagled to a large rock outcropping.

"Missy, do you think you can restrain yourself until I return with the others?"

"They'll be ready for your return, and I'll be ready to be your queen."

"Good, and throw some water on Julianna to wake her up. I wouldn't want her to miss the show. You can play with her all you want while I'm gone. Consider it a reward for keeping watch over my little Initiate while I was at college. Unmarked though, remember!"

Julianna heard his footfalls departing through the woods.

"We'll wake her up in a minute or two," Missy said. "I'm sure Shane wouldn't mind one bit if I have some fun with you too. Are you as slutty as your sister, Lorelei?"

"Stop touching me!" Lorelei yelled.

"Did your big sister ever tell you how I was the first to see her naked? She was so juicy and ripe."

"Ouch, what is wrong with you, perv? Leave me alone!"

"Hey, bitch! Shane's gonna kick your ass if you hurt my sister," Julianna shouted.

"Oh my, sleeping beauty is still alive, what a shame."

Julianna cackled. "God, you're so pathetic! Is there any guy you wouldn't screw to get ahead? Everybody knows you like girls, always did, but I guess you're a switch hitter if it proves to your advantage. You really think Shane is going to make you his queen? He told me he has someone else in mind for the job."

"Who?"

"I'll never tell, but it sure isn't you!"

"Who was it?" Missy was suddenly standing in front of her.

"Fuck you!" Julianna drove her knee into the other woman's stomach.

Missy growled, and Julianna saw the sharp edges of her teeth.

"It won't go so well for you this time, Indian girl. You don't have any friends here to protect you. And I owe you. Shane will understand. Did you know you broke my nose that day at the river, squaw slut?"

“Poor baby. All talk, no action.” Julianna threw a kick at her. Missy stepped aside, grabbed Julianna’s ankle, and bit down on it.

“Ah, shit!” Julianna said, even as her other foot slammed into the back of Missy’s head.

Missy grabbed Julianna at the knees and drove her into the pole she was tied to, then moved towards her neck, her jaws opened wide. Julianna squirmed sideways, but the rope pulled her up short.

Missy’s nails ripped through her blouse and drew blood, but her claws got caught in the chain of the turquoise pendant. Julianna tried to knee her, but she was too close. Again, her jaws stretched wide, and the stench of rotted meat, the smell of death, flooded the space between them. Missy’s teeth glistened in the faint light. *She’s nearly changed!* Missy’s teeth sank into her left breast.

The searing pain drove the breath from her. Julianna sucked at the air to recover, and fought the darkness trying to consume her.

Missy smiled with a mouth full of daggers. “Look at what you made me do,” she growled, took a long lick of Julianna’s blood, and turned back toward Lorelei.

Julianna fought back the horrific implications of being bitten by a werewolf and continued her taunts. “Leave her alone, you little pansy poodle bitch. You don’t amount to a hair on a real dog’s ass. I’m not finished with you yet, mutt-face.”

The Missy beast turned and charged. Julianna lifted her thighs at the hips and kicked out with both feet, catching Missy’s extended jaw, sending her to the ground.

Julianna heard someone behind her and swiveled her head to face the new opponent. “Jase? What are you…?”

“No time.” He cut the ropes with a machete. “Untie Lorelei. I’ll take care of this monster.”

"No," Julianna said, and pulled the machete from his hands. "She's mine!" *Have to end the curse before it begins!*

Missy howled, scrambled to her feet, and charged, claws out and teeth bared. Julianna waited until the last second, twisted, and stuck out her leg. The momentum of the werewolf threw it in a somersault to the ground. Julianna was on the wolf in an instant and swung the machete. Blood spurted from the beast's neck, covering Julianna's face and chest.

The Missy wolf attempted one weak howl, and Julianna swung her machete again, severing the wolfish head.

"I should have done that a long time ago, bitch. Lorelei, are you all right?"

"I can't get these things untied. I need the machete." Jase said.

"Shit, you only brought one?"

"We were in kind of a hurry."

Then the howls from the dogs of hell surrounded them.

# Chapter Forty-Two

Chase hurried from the cabin, trying to keep on the trail while it was still fresh, but Shane hadn't expended much effort to conceal his movements. He was either hurried, overconfident, or stupid, any of which might play to Chase's advantage.

Where was he taking Julianna? The drag marks stopped, and the trail became harder to follow. Shane must have switched to carrying her. Their general direction headed toward the road, and Chase moved across the road and circled, searching for sign on the other side. He found where Shane put Julianna down, and two sets of footprints continued on.

He moved forward at a trot, sometimes too fast, and he needed to circle back to where he lost the trail. *Slow down, Chase. Take the time to read the sign. What did Thane say about tracking? The first one to the finish line doesn't win if the finish line is the wrong one.*

There was sign, a small bent branch on a spicebush, and some disturbance in the leaves on the ground. Ah! Julianna's footprints…no, they weren't Julianna's shoes. How did he miss the high heel indentation? Julianna wouldn't be caught dead in anything so impractical.

*Go, Chase, just move.* Julianna was still unconscious then…she might even be dead, he thought. No, not that. That was the one scenario he wouldn't consider, couldn't consider, not if he was to continue functioning.

*Julianna, where are you?* Chase saw the next track in some disturbed leaves and bent down to get a better look. He heard a rustling in front of him. Shane and Julianna? He knelt behind a massive sycamore tree and listened.

Wolves! Two to his left front, another to his right, and several now following his trail. Too many for him to fight. Julianna's safety depended on him, so he couldn't rush in like a fool. He slipped down the bank to a small mountain spring and pulled off his shirt. He gouged out some dark mud from the spring's source and rubbed it over his face and under his arms. He reached down to apply it generously to his crotch. A small eastern cedar tree provided additional scent camouflage.

He climbed up into the sycamore and surveyed his surroundings. He saw the two lead Wolfen climb a small hill and point toward the rock outcroppings called The Devil's Knuckles. The larger wolf had a prominent grey-haired scar at his forehead. Malcolm! The odds were good that the younger blond wolf was Shane, and if so, what did he do with Julianna?

There was minimal movement at the Knuckles, but Chase could make out a body sprawled on the ground. Julianna? The Wolfen, in varying degrees of transformation, moved toward the rocks.

The two wolves on the hill moved forward together. Then Malcolm's wolf pointed at the Knuckles again, slapped his chest, and then pushed the blond wolf backwards. The smaller wolf at first cowered as a submissive dog might, then strode past with his Wolfen head held high. Malcolm raised his foot, and gave the blond wolf a shove.

But the younger beast suddenly leapt up and sank his teeth in Malcolm's throat. He shook his head from side to side, and ripped loose a chunk of bloody flesh. He threw back his head and swallowed the meat with a gulp. He howled and raced to the front of the pack.

# Chapter Forty-Three

Julianna wacked off a sapling and sharpened the end into a makeshift spear. She tossed it to Jase and quickly cut another.

"Be right there, Lorelei," she said.

"Umm, Julianna? Maybe she'll be safer the way she is. What if she runs off with them? She's nearly turned."

She turned toward her sister, and saw her writhing, her mouth foaming. "I don't know Jase, but I can't leave her defenseless."

A muscular blond-haired wolf pushed through the brush, sniffed at Missy, and howled. Several more wolves joined the first, on all fours, their sunken eyes glowing yellow, boring into Julianna. She and Jase backed up to the rock that held Lorelei.

"Keep between the dogs and Lorelei," Julianna said.

The blond Wolfen smiled at her then, or made a mockery of a human smile at least. Drool dripped from its needle-sharp teeth in anticipation. It licked its chops. The set of its eyes and the wavy blond fur could only mean one thing.

"Shane! Bring it on, you fucker!" Julianna held her spear in front of her.

The wolf flexed its muscles, crouched down, and hurtled toward her. Julianna squatted, anchored the blunt end of the spear to the ground, and braced for impact. A blur of ratty copper fur flashed by and rammed the Shane beast in the side.

Shapeless, torn flesh hung from the attacking beast's crotch, a bleeding, swollen pustule. *Garret!*

The beast snapped at the Shane-wolf's jugular, but Shane's forearm deflected the attack, and Garret's fangs chomped down on his shoulder.

The violent battle for control of the pack distracted the other wolves for but a moment. As the two Alpha contenders rolled on the ground, clawing and biting, the others turned back toward their prey.

A red-furred wolf reared up on its hind legs and howled. It darted toward Lorelei, tossing Jase aside much as a child whacking down his toy army men. The beast shoved his cold wet snout between Lorelei's legs. The wolf in her responded, thrusting her hips upward, panting in anticipation.

Jase threw one of the spears, impaling the beast in the center of its chest. It fell backwards and wriggled like a freshly pinned specimen in a bug collection. The other wolf circled cautiously as two more entered the clearing.

"We can't just stand here and hope to pick them off one by one, and the machete is all the silver we have," Julianna said. "Sooner or later their little canine brains will decide to rush us."

"I know." Jase thrust his other spear into a beast's throat. "But we can't leave Lor, and we can't turn her loose either."

"Maybe we can." Julianna rushed one of the werewolves. She swung her blade and gashed its thigh, but its return swat clawed across her back, ripping through her shirt into her skin. Julianna fell in a somersault and landed on her feet behind the fighting brother wolves. Engaged in their own battle for dominance, they didn't notice her until her machete struck Shane's skull, then she lunged it at Garret's torso. The blade sunk beneath his ribcage up to the hilt.

Leaderless and confused, with their tails tucked, the two subordinate wolves growled and backed slowly into the woods to regroup. Julianna ran to her sister and cut the ropes holding her down, but left her hands tied together.

"I'm sorry, Sis. You stick tight to me and Jase until the wolf wears off. I'm trusting you."

Lorelei nodded her head.

"I'm not sure that's a good idea, Julianna." Jase said.

"This isn't a defensible position, and unless I miss my guess, one of Shane's family is responsible for your and Lorelei's curse. Malcolm is the only one still out there, and we have to take the chance. Let's move. They'll get organized again soon."

*Chase, where are you?*

# Chapter Forty-Four

Chase descended from his perch in the sycamore and slipped toward the hill where Malcolm met his fate moments before. The old wolf's throat, ripped away by Shane's fangs, gaped open to his neck bones. *One less werewolf. Julianna!*

The sound of fighting at Devil's Knuckles carried to Chase, and he ran toward the fray without scenting the air or checking for sign. Twice he tripped over hidden rocks. The second one sent him flying off of a rocky ledge. Rocks smashed into his chest on the way down, and his knee impacted a large oak root at the bottom.

"Damn!" His chest and knee on fire, he managed to climb back up and limp on. *Julianna!*

He crested the hill to the Knuckles, saw the blood bath. What he assumed to be Shane and another wolf were entwined in each other's arms, in a perversely grotesque embrace. Shane's ear, the one with the golden earring, hung off of his skull, resembling a hound's ear rather than a wolf's. Chunks of flesh were torn from Garret's body, a wound seeped blood from his chest, and his groin, oozing and covered with green flies…Chase had to look away. A third wolf twisted on the ground, facing the moon, its claws pawing at the long stake protruding from its chest. Chase slammed his machete down on its skull and walked on.

*Look for the sign,* he thought. *Figure this out.* He examined the disturbed battleground and counted the different paw prints encircling the large rock. Cut ropes dangled from its blood-stained surface. Whose blood?

A faint trail of fresh blood led away from the clearing. An injured wolf, or one of his loved ones? He spotted three sets of tracks moving in the opposite direction, back toward the cabin. *Julianna, Jase and Lorelei… they have to be close.*

From the numbers of wolves he'd seen in the woods, Chase knew some remained behind after the Spring Gathering to exact vengeance for their losses. How could they kill them all?

*Fuck it, kill or be killed*, he thought, and dashed into the woods.

# Chapter Forty-Five

Julianna and her two companions ran towards the cabin, hoping the defenses there would hold. A place to make their last stand against the rest of the wolves. Why were there so many? That they wouldn't follow didn't cross her mind. They had hurt the wolves, two of their leaders were killed. And the three of them still ran free. The mongrels wouldn't be able to resist.

They crossed a small feeder stream, halfway home, when the howls began anew. Lorelei stopped abruptly, then turned back toward the sound with a look of yearning.

"Damn it! Run, Lorelei! Now!" Jase ordered.

Lorelei moaned softly, then spun around and followed Jase.

By the time the trio reached the cabin, the sounds of many padded feet closed on their heels, and Jase and Julianna dragged Lorelei forward. Julianna threw open the front door.

"Bar the windows, Jase, and bolt the door." Julianna ran to retrieve more weapons from Lorelei's closet arsenal. She slipped a pistol and her bloodied machete into her belt and slung a rifle over her shoulder. Carrying another silver-coated machete, a shotgun, and boxes of ammo, she hurried back to the living room. She dropped a box of shells at Jase's feet and handed him the shotgun and machete.

"Make every shot count," she said.

Lorelei growled and sprinted down the hallway with Julianna in close pursuit, afraid her sister's wolf blood overwhelmed her common sense. Lorelei ran to her mother's room and yanked on the closet door, splintering the trim. She dove in, clothes and shoes tossed carelessly behind her. She turned to Julianna and pointed to a small wooden box marked "Explosives."

"Dynamite!" Julianna kissed her sister's fuzzy cheek. She grabbed a box and headed for the front room until she heard a scratching at her bedroom door. She paused, and slowly opened it. Xena bounded out.

"Jesus, you scared me, Xena! I forgot about you, baby, but you better stay in my room."

Jase waited in the living room, staring out into the darkness. Julianna walked to the front door and rested her finger on the switch to the outside flood light.

"Ready, Jase?"

"Ready as I'll ever be."

Julianna flipped the switch and gasped at the circle of yellow eyes reflecting back at them.

"How many do you count?" Julianna moved to the kitchen window.

"Too many."

Julianna smashed the window glass with the butt of her rifle, took careful aim between two glowing yellow eyes, and slowly squeezed the trigger. The eyes disappeared, and an answering shot echoed from Jase's shotgun. Again and again they fired at targets. Lorelei huddled in the corner nearest her sister, trembling like a gun-shy rabbit hound.

The circle of wolves closed in, becoming more brazen, or desperate. One made a rush at the porch. Jase's shot clipped its arm, but it vaulted easily to the roof. Clawed feet scratched at the shingles.

"How much ammo do you have left? Do we have enough?" Jase yelled.

"It depends on how many are still out there." Julianna pried open the wooden box and grabbed a stick of dynamite.

"Maybe this will chase them off for a while, at least. When I light the fuse, open the door, cover me and slam it shut as soon as I get back in. Okay?"

Jase nodded his head, and Julianna struck the match, lit the fuse, and then ran toward the door. Jase threw it open as she cocked her arm back to throw. Lorelei leapt from her crouch in the corner, ramming into Julianna as she raced through the open door. The dynamite slipped to the floor, spitting sparks, and rolled away towards Jase.

"Dammit, Lorelei!" Julianna yelled. Jase snatched up the explosive, and slung the short-fused dynamite stick with all he had through the door, away from the direction Lorelei ran.

The explosion rocked the walls of the cabin and tossed its occupants to the wood floor. Julianna couldn't hear anything over the ringing in her ears. She crawled to the window and peered out.

"I don't see their eyes anymore. But I think you just blew up our well. Which way did Lorelei go?"

"What?"

"Which way did…"

"I can't hear you."

"I'm going after Lorelei!" she yelled into his ear. "Get back to the window!"

# Chapter Forty-Six

Their location was obvious now. No need to follow sign; he just had to head toward the shooting. And in that direction sat the cabin, over the next rise.

His heart thundered in his chest as he limped on, but he increased his pace over the rough, ankle-breaking terrain. He considered evaluating the scene before dashing in from the woods, but the thought reminded him of that vulture poster: *Fuck patience. I'm gonna kill something.* Julianna was close, and she needed him.

He leapt into the clearing without breaking stride, ready for anything, except the earth jarring boom that knocked him off his feet and planted him face first in the dirt.

"What the hell?"

He got to his knees, noting with detachment the many superficial wounds opened by the flying dirt and sand from the explosion. He stood, shakily, and trotted on toward the cabin. He heard muffled noises in the woods behind him, unsure if the explosion caused loss of his hearing, or if the encroachment of the wolves was more cautious now.

He looked from side to side as he ran and saw brush moving to the left of the cabin, but he was distracted by a crouching wolf on the cabin's roof. He drew his pistol, took a bead, and pulled the trigger. The young wolf dropped in a heap to the porch. Chase reached for his machete as he holstered his gun, but another wolf plowed into his side, knocking him off his feet.

Chase landed hard, lost his breath, and gasped at the air. The blond-furred attacker kicked him in the back, its claws raking across his skin. He rolled out of the way of the second kick and reached for his holster. Empty! Chase scrambled on the ground, looking for his firearm in the dim light from the cabin. The wolf bent down until its ghastly teeth were inches from Chase's nose, flooding his olfactory sense with its sour fetid breath. The beast growled in pleasure and stood up to its full height. One mangled ear dangled to its chin.

"Shane! I thought you were dead. No matter, you soon will be!

Wolves crept from the woods and encircled the two enemies with blood lust flaming in their eyes. Shane's wolf growled again and held up his arms, signaling his followers to stay.

"Want me all for yourself, do you?" Chase jumped up, reached behind his back, and pulled the machete from its sheath. "Come and get it!"

Shane lunged for his throat, but Chase dove forward and head-butted the beast. Its head jerked backwards, and Chase twisted, then swept his blade up and across the beast's abdomen.

Shane dropped to all fours and Chase drew back both arms for a fatal head blow. But Shane swung his hind legs in a sweeping arc, and his claws snagged Chase behind his knee. As Chase fell, the wolf snapped his jaws on a mouthful of shirt. It drew Chase closer, then lurched forward and snapped again. Chase felt hot pain as the wolf's teeth sank into his side. Shane lifted his head, and shook Chase like a rag doll, dropped him to the ground, and stood over him, sniffing. His snout pushed against Chase's still form, as if urging him to play some more.

Chase's body was racked with pain. Had he passed out for a moment? Without opening his eyes, he knew the huge beast hovered over him, waiting. Its breath hung in the air like forgotten shrimp shells in the trash can. He needed to know what parts of his body he could still depend on, and took a moment to assess the damage by determining the parts that didn't hurt. His ears were all he could come up with.

The Shane-wolf growled softly at his throat, and Chase froze. His eyes opened a sliver. Shane threw his head back and howled. Now or never, he thought, and with all his remaining strength, drove his machete into Shane's gullet. The wolf's warm blood drenched him with its spray.

Chase managed to get his knees under him, swung the machete, and severed the beast's head. It rolled on the ground and came to rest, its eyes staring sightlessly at the moon.

"Sit. Stay. Good boy." Using his blade for support, he forced himself to stand. Yellow eyes surrounded him, closing in. Chase bent down, picked a branch, and tossed it over the wolves' heads.

"Fetch!" he yelled. One juvenile wolf's eyes actually followed the flight of the stick, but the others snarled, and their lips peeled back to reveal their fangs.

"Shit. You can't blame a guy for trying. C'mon then, pooches. Let's see what you've got."

The wolves advanced, heads low and growling. Their haunches dropped as they prepared to pounce. Chase waved his machete back and forth, and then heard the cabin door open. A shot rang out and whizzed over his head.

"Chase!" Julianna screamed.

Man and beasts all turned toward the sound, unmoving. But when the naked woman rushed out of the trees with a wolf on her heels, the race began.

# Chapter Forty-Seven

"I heard a shot. Did you hear it?" Julianna stared out the window.

"Yeah, and I hope it's a battalion of reinforcements," Jase said.

"Better than that, it's Chase…Chase is coming."

She checked the cartridges in her rifle, and then filled the clip. She followed suit with her pistol, and then slipped the machete into its sheath on her back. She cut a long strip off of her leather jacket, wrapped two thicknesses around her neck, and then tied them together under her chin.

"Dog bite protection," she said in answer to the question in Jase's face.

"Julianna, I think I should be the one…"

"Which way did she go?"

Jase pointed in the direction he'd last seen Lorelei running. "I need to be the one to go. Stay here, and cover me."

"Those are my woods out there. I've known them since I was a child. My sister too, so my fight. You stay, you cover. Ready?"

"Chase will kick my ass if I let you go, Jules!"

"Let's hope we all live to see that." She smiled, then threw open the door and ran into the night.

Chase stood in the front yard surrounded by a half dozen mature wolves. In one eye blink, she noted his bloody clothes, and the limp way he held his body. She shot over the beasts' heads, and then screamed Chase's name.

The wolves turned their full attention on her.

"Bring it, bitches," she said under her breath. But the wolves suddenly turned away from her, and she snapped her head around to follow their gaze.

"Lorelei!" Julianna ran to intercept her sister, as did the wolves. Chase followed with a pronounced limp. A barrage of shots echoed from the cabin, and wolves fell in agony.

Julianna reached Lorelei first and threw her to the dirt as the first wolf sprang. Julianna stood her ground and slashed the beast's throat as it sailed over her. The second wolf bowled her over, but two rapid-fire shots in the chest knocked the beast down. It crawled on towards Lorelei, snapping its massive jaws.

"Lorelei!" She tossed the machete to her, and then snapped off another round into the head of a beast rushing her.

Its momentum carried it on, knocking her backwards, and landing squarely on top of her. In its death throes, it swung its head and clicked its teeth. Her arms were bent beneath the wolf, but her hands were on its neck, holding back the dreadful fangs. She felt the animal quiver, then heard its death moan as it fell limp in her hands.

"Get off of me!" The dead wolf's fur filled her nose and mouth. She pushed and prodded at the beast. Her breath came in gasps, and she fought herself for control. *Don't lose it now, Jules.*

With her one uncovered eye, she saw a lone black wolf approach slowly, and she played dead. A low pitched growl purred from its throat, and Julianna flinched. The wolf stuck its cold wet snout into her eye, and tried to close its jaws on her head. But there wasn't enough of it exposed, and the wolf's dagger teeth slipped off the skull, tearing open Julianna's scalp. The beast wiggled its jaws under the dead wolf, and this time found purchase, as it sunk its teeth into her shoulder. Julianna screamed in pain and anguish. *Not again!* She held on to the belly hairs of the dead wolf as the black one, with its hold on her shoulder, tried to drag her out.

The wolf dragged both of them, but for every foot they slid together, Julianna slid out a bit from under the dead beast. She felt her butt cheeks rubbing on the rocky ground and knew the wolf was winning the tug of war. When her head and shoulders were free, Julianna wiggled her arms, but couldn't free them from the weight of the dead Wolfen. The black one released its hold on her shoulder and examined its prize, sniffing her, licking her mouth.

She heard Lorelei yell something that made no sense to her, something from a conversation long ago.

The wolf seemed to smile, and its cavernous jaws stretched opened for the kill.

"Go to hell, mutt!" Julianna closed her eyes and waited for the end.

*I trust you, Chase. Take care of my sister.*

# Chapter Forty-Eight

Lorelei snatched the machete that Julianna tossed to her and deftly split open the crawling wolf's head. She saw Chase fighting his way toward them, slashing through the wolves that stood in his way, and they fell like bowling pins on a Saturday night…but where did Julianna go?

Growling, snapping werewolves filled the night air with the howls of pursuit and the yelps of pain. Everything was happening so fast. Her transition left her in a mental fog, and she shook her head to clear the mud from her brain.

"Get a grip, girl, or you're dead," she told herself.

Lorelei clutched the machete's handle and moved forward to Julianna's last position. Where the hell was she? From under a mass of wolf fur, she heard her sister's voice, clear and strong.

"Go to hell, mutt!"

Then Lorelei saw the black wolf. She didn't need to think now. Instinct took over as she jumped to her sister's aid. The wolf popped its teeth at Julianna in anticipation of the kill, and threw open its maw. Lorelei grabbed the big wolf's tail and yanked. It growled, but didn't budge.

She retained her hold with one hand, swung her machete with the other, and lopped off its tail at the root. The dark wolf squealed in pain.

"Hey, Lassie, this is for you!" Lorelei drew back her blade to strike again.

The wolf's head snapped back, and she heard a squishy, cracking pop as the tip of Chase's machete sprouted between the beast's ears. Lorelei's machete clanged as it met Chase's inside the beast's skull.

Together, Lorelei and Chase pulled the Wolfen off of Julianna. Her face was covered in wolf blood and her own. She didn't move.

"Is she breathing?" Lorelei asked, gently slapping her sister's cheek.

Julianna's eyes flew open. "I'm not dead?"

"Not today." Chase drew her to her feet and held her in his arms.

# Chapter Forty-Nine

"Do you think we got them all?" Jase yelled, and ran toward them from the house.

"I think so, I think they're done," Chase said.

A brilliant violet and red sunrise greeted them as they limped their way back to the cabin. Showering off the drying blood breathed a semblance of new life into them, and Lorelei put on a pot of coffee. Their wounds and sprains were disinfected, wrapped, and bandaged by the time the coffee was ready, and they sat heavily in the dining room chairs, tired but too adrenalized to sleep.

Chase smiled at Jase and Lorelei holding hands on top of the table.

"And how is it that my brother ran around all night, under a full moon, and was only a bit furrier than usual? How did you stop the transformation?" Chase asked.

"The potion!" Jase and Lorelei answered together and laughed.

"It worked great, but it sure leaves you with a bad hangover," Jase added.

Julianna poured everyone's coffee, adding to each a splash of bourbon, then sat at Chase's side. She told them how Shane turned the tables on her by slipping a drug into her wine. "Missy was there too, Chase. Remember the bitch Missy?"

"Yes, I remember. I'll bet she was the headless, prissy-looking one up on the Knuckles. Well done. I guess our plan of attack wasn't quite as foolproof as we thought." Chase took a sip of coffee and frowned.

"It was good enough, though, and we still ended up with the desired results. Didn't some famous idiot say the end justifies the means?" Julianna asked.

"Yeah, but tomorrow the real fun starts – getting rid of all those desired results, the several tons of dead wolf in the yard," Jase said.

"And the ones up at Devil's Knuckles, don't forget. And there's a really big Alpha wolf on a hillside near there with its throat ripped out." Chase then shared the story of how he'd watched from the top of the sycamore tree while Shane killed his father.

"So, what the hell happened to you, Lorelei? Running off like that. I should beat your ass," Julianna said.

"That might not be the only ass-whipping coming, but it will have to wait. I'm too tired tonight," Chase said.

"Well someone might need a spanking, but it ain't me." Jase pointed his thumb at Julianna and laughed. "I tried to stop her, Chase, but that is one hardheaded woman."

"She definitely is that," Lorelei chimed in.

"Oh no, you're not getting out of this by turning the spotlight on me. What were you thinking running out of here with half of the Wolfen in the state waiting for you in our yard?"

"I wasn't, Jules. Thinking, that is. I heard the howls of the pack and the passion of their voices. This overwhelming urge for their freedom surged in me, and before I knew it, a wolf had me on the ground ready to have its way with me."

"You sure that wasn't the urge you were feeling?" Julianna asked.

Lorelei dropped her eyes to the floor, and her cheeks flushed red. "I wouldn't have fought it."

"It's nothing to be ashamed of. It was the curse. Believe me, I understand the pull it has on a person, but how did you get away? When we saw you streaking naked across the front yard?" Jase gave her a twisted smile. "That would have been a scene I played over and over in my mind forever, by the way, if it wasn't for the furry monstrosity chasing you."

"I only got away because males, human or wolf, are all the same. They never outgrow their schoolyard mentality and can't miss out on seeing a good fight. Don't shake your head, Jase. Seems that Malcolm's entire bloodline had to be killed for my curse to die. It wasn't until Chase killed Shane that I changed back. And I mean fast, and just in time. I suddenly realized my naked butt was sticking up in the air, and something heavy and fuzzy had a solid grip on my hips. I was pretty addle-brained, but it didn't take an Einstein to figure out what was going to happen next. I twisted around and punched him in the jaw."

"You're lucky he didn't rip out your throat!" Julianna said.

"I thought that too, but it wasn't luck at all. When the wolf heard all the shouting, howling, and shooting, it jumped off me and ran toward the fight. I took off running back to the cabin, and the younger one chased me. Can you imagine that?" She looked at Jase.

"Imagine what? That a young male anything chased you? I don't have any trouble believing that at all," Jase said and grinned.

"No." Lorelei stood up, turned her back to Jase, and winked at him over her shoulder. She bent over and lightly slapped herself on the butt. "Can you believe the other wolf turned this down?"

Julianna laughed. "God, you are such a damn tease."

Lorelei's eyes never left Jase's as she said, "I am no tease." She turned around and offered Jase her hand. "If you two will please excuse us?" She led Jase to her room.

Lorelei's door slammed shut, but it did not filter out her giggles, soon followed by her squeals, and ending some time later with her muted sighs.

Chase and Julianna attempted conversation throughout it all, keeping their voices high to provide their siblings a degree of privacy and modesty. But then the bedsprings started squeaking a second time, and Lorelei's voice rose and filled the small cabin. "Oh Jase!

They stared at their hands on the table in silence. Chase looked up, and Julianna smiled back at him sheepishly, biting her lip. Then Lorelei yelled "Oh yeah, Jase!" And Chase lost all self-control. A torrent of pent up laughter ripped from his throat, and he fell to his knees on the floor, laughing to the point of tears.

"Hush, Chase, stop it, they'll hear you."

"Sorry, but I'm trying."

"Well, *they* aren't exactly trying to be quiet, I agree!" Julianna joined in the laughter.

"Come on then." Chase took her hand and kissed it. His fingernails lightly scratched her back and his other hand squeezed a butt cheek. "Let's go make some noises of our own."

Julianna dropped her eyes to the floor. "I'm pretty beat up, Chase. I don't have the super-Wolfen healing abilities the rest of you share."

"I'm sorry, Julianna. I wasn't thinking…"

Julianna looked up, her eyes mirroring her smile as she took his hand and pulled him toward the bedroom. "Would you just hold me, my love, with nothing between us?"

"I'll do anything and be anything you want, Julianna."

Clothes were hitting the floor before they were halfway down the hall.

"God, you are beautiful," Chase said.

"Even with all the bandages?"

"Yeah, you're sexy as hell."

"Hurry up, Chase. I want to be in your arms – to feel safe for the first time in a long time."

"I can't think of anywhere I'd rather be, Julianna. I'd spend every moment for the rest of my life in your embrace."

She grinned. "Well, if you play your cards right, I might keep you around – for a week or two anyway."

He chuckled. "Now, don't get all bitchy."

"After tonight, Chase, if you ever call me a bitch, I'll personally beat that sweet ass of yours!" She smirked and rolled over onto her stomach. "Unless that's what you want?"

Chase tossed the last of his clothes to the floor, and nibbled on her upturned right cheek. "And what do *you* want, my love?"

"I want you, Chase. Anything, anywhere, anytime, as long as it's with you."

# Epilogue

Chase and Julianna returned to the university together after their missed semester. Julianna finished her degree in Anthropology, with a minor in Mythology. Chase graduated with a degree in Archaeology.

Before they married, their degrees earned them teaching positions at the local high school, with guest lecturer status at the community college. They reside at Julianna's old cabin, where so many memories were made, some good, some not, but all a part of who they are. Their love of the woods and the river, and for each other, affords them great pleasure, but whenever they're in the least bit bored, they take a trip to visit their siblings.

Lorelei and Jase aren't the easiest people to locate, but they can be found, if someone with an inquisitive nature knows the sort of places to search. Usually, that means in the hills near some small town in West Virginia, far from the beaten path of the main roads. They follow the headlines and Internet reports of animal maulings, or any vicious, grisly deaths. Always in pursuit of their old enemies, those who held their youth in chains.

Xena lived happily ever after.

THE END

# About Davina Guy

Davina calls the fields and rivers of Southern Maryland home, and studied at UMUC while serving overseas with the US Army. When not writing, the author enjoys hiking, gardening and kayaking down the South Branch of the Potomac River in West Virginia. Davina is the pseudonym used by author D. Thompson for romance novels.

**Social Media Links**

e-mail: DavinaGuy1@gmail.com

Facebook:
https://www.facebook.com/profile.php?id=100018246195386

Twitter: https://twitter.com/davinaguy75 Guy@davinaguy75

www.ingramcontent.com/pod-product-compliance
Lightning Source LLC
Chambersburg PA
CBHW051134020726
47501CB00005B/1499

* 9 7 8 1 6 2 5 2 6 7 2 1 4 *